Ross opened her camera, deftly removed the film

"What the hell do you think you're doing?" Camilla asked in horror as he exposed the whole length of the film.

"No one takes photographs in my house without my permission." He was unrepentant.

"You had no right to do that!" Camilla seethed.

"Only part of that film was shot in your house. The rest were scenes I took on the way here." She glared at him. "All you had to do was ask and I wouldn't have used the ones of the house. I suppose you're unfamiliar with such civilized procedures."

"I'm not used to asking for my rights. I prefer to take them," Ross said. "I'd advise you to bear that in mind when dealing with me."

Stephanie Howard is a British author whose
two ambitions since childhood were to see the
world and write. Her first venture into the world
was a four-year stay in Italy, learning the language
and supporting herself by writing short stories.
Then her sensible side brought her back to London
to read Social Administrations at the London
School of Economics. She has held various editorial
posts at magazines such as *Reader's Digest*, *Vanity
Fair*, *Women's Own*, as well as writing free-lance
for *Cosmopolitan*, *Good Housekeeping* and *The
Observer*. However, she has spent the past six
years happily trotting around the globe. Last year
she returned to the U.K. to write romance novels.

Books by Stephanie Howard

HARLEQUIN PRESENTS
1098—RELUCTANT PRISONER
1130—DARK LUCIFER
1168—HIGHLAND TURMOIL
1273—BRIDE FOR A PRICE
1307—KISS OF THE FALCON

Don't miss any of our special offers. Write to us at the
following address for information on our newest releases.

Harlequin Reader Service
901 Fuhrmann Blvd., P.O. Box 1397, Buffalo, NY 14240
Canadian address: P.O. Box 603,
Fort Erie, Ont. L2A 5X3

MASTER OF
GLEN CRANNACH

Stephanie Howard

Harlequin Books

TORONTO • NEW YORK • LONDON
AMSTERDAM • PARIS • SYDNEY • HAMBURG
STOCKHOLM • ATHENS • TOKYO • MILAN

Original hardcover edition published in 1990
by Mills & Boon Limited

ISBN 0-373-03093-2

Harlequin Romance first edition December 1990
Harlequin Romance second edition January 1991

CHAPTER ONE

CAMILLA came hammering round the woodland bend like a bat out of hell and very nearly went ploughing straight into a flock of black-faced sheep.

Just in time, with a muttered curse, she slammed her foot down hard on the brake and brought the car to a tyre-splitting halt. 'Blast and damnation!' she seethed, making a quick check over her shoulder to ensure that her precious camera-bag was safe. Then, satisfied, she turned her attention to the spectacle before her. 'This just about crowns the whole ruddy lot!'

The road ahead was completely blocked by a solid woolly mass, which appeared not to have the remotest intention of thoughtfully moving out of her way. It was the last straw. The final, fatal frustration in a day which had started out badly, then proceeded to get progressively worse.

It was less than three hours since Camilla had flown into Inverness from London on a supposedly routine photographic assignment, and already she was totally convinced of something she had suspected right from the start—that she and the Highlands of Scotland were destined to make uneasy bedmates. Three hours had already been more than enough. How would she ever survive a whole *week*?

In a gesture that gave vent to all her pent-up

frustration, she banged her fist down hard on the horn.

It was a foolish, and potentially dangerous thing to do. Even before the blast rang out, disturbing the peaceful country air and sending a visible ripple of alarm through the nervous, huddled flock. Camilla realised her mistake.

But she was not prepared for the reaction it brought.

'What the hell do you think you're doing?' All at once, a furious male voice was bellowing at her, making her swing round guiltily in her seat to face the tall, powerfully-built figure in thick Aran sweater and body-hugging jeans who was striding impatiently towards her through the trees on the opposite side of the road.

As he moved, the head of thick, dark hair blew back, away from his face, revealing a set of striking features, handsomely proportioned, yet carved from stone. And, judging by the harsh, uncompromising lines in which those features were currently set, it was not difficult to ascertain the mood that prevailed in the psyche beyond. Even at this relatively safe distance, the ground seemed to tremble at his approach.

In a couple of athletic bounds, he had emerged from the trees and leapt down on to the road. 'Where the hell do you think you are—Brand's Hatch?' he demanded. 'This road isn't a racetrack, you know! And are you out of your bloody mind, banging on your horn like that?'

The apology that had been hovering politely on Camilla's lips dissolved with the icy rapidity of a snowflake in a mountain stream. Who the devil did this wild-looking, ill-mannered individual think he was, to dare to speak to her like that?

Her spine stiffened perceptibly as, very slowly and deliberately, she began to wind her window down. Then, defiantly tossing an errant strand of pale blonde hair across her shoulder, she narrowed her eyes imperiously, leaned out and, totally ignoring his boorish demands, enquired in a cutting voice, 'Are you, by any chance, in charge of these animals?'

'And if I am?'

As he paused to issue the challenge in a tone quite as cutting as her own, thumbs hooked belligerently in the pockets of his narrow, thigh-hugging jeans, broad shoulders beneath the chunky sweater thrown back aggressively, he had crossed the narrow distance between them and was virtually standing over the car.

And as Camilla squinted up anxiously into the arresting, deeply tanned face, with its fiercely penetrating iron-grey eyes, dark brows, strong nose and wide, passionate mouth, she was aware that the air around him seemed to shiver with a sense of immense power held in check.

But she was not about to be intimidated by some upstart farm-hand, however overpowering his presence might be! With difficulty, she held his gaze—those eyes were the eyes of a hunter, she sensed—and forced herself to snap right back, 'Then I would suggest that you do a better job of keeping them under control! They happen to be blocking my path!'

'Blocking your path? Dear, dear, we can't have that.' He raised one dark eyebrow in amused sarcasm and a caustic smile touched the granite-carved lips. Then all pretence at humour abruptly left his face as he added, evidently picking up her southern accent, 'You're not in the middle of Knightsbridge now, you know. I'm afraid in these parts different rules apply.'

Too right! thought Camilla with bitter irony, remembering the late arrival of her flight, the mix-up about the hire car at the airport and her total failure so far to elicit even marginally comprehensible directions to her ultimate destination, the remote and apparently inaccessible castle at Glen Crannach. The civilised rules of London's Knightsbridge were most definitely not in evidence here. Rules of chaos and disorder, it seemed, prevailed!

Wisdom, however, cautioned her to keep such observations to herself as the wild-looking, raven-haired creature in the Aran sweater went on to enlighten her, 'In this part of the world, I'm afraid, animals of the four-legged variety are considered to have as much right to use the highways as their two-legged cousins and their cars.'

'How touchingly egalitarian!' Camilla glared her impatience at him through angry, long-lashed, china-blue eyes. An unaccustomed frown of exasperation marred her normally good-humoured face. 'Then perhaps you wouldn't mind explaining to me how this particular two-legged animal, and her car, are supposed to get where they're going to when a herd of her four-legged cousins are so inconsiderately blocking the way?'

Another fleeting smile of amusement briefly touched the wide, sensuous lips as the stranger deliberately took pleasure in carefully correcting her. 'Flock, not herd.' Then, as she frowned at him, momentarily uncomprehending, he elaborated condescendingly, 'I realise you don't have sheep in Knightsbridge—at least, not of the variety under discussion here—but the correct terminology for a group of such animals happens to be flock, not herd.'

The normally serene blue eyes flashed jaggedly, like chipped porcelain. She had not just flown over six hundred miles and driven another fifty or more for a lesson in farm etiquette. Nor, even less, to be the butt of this insufferable upstart's humour. Acidly, she informed him, 'I don't give a damn about the correct terminology! All I want is for you to move the wretched things out of my way!'

'Oh, is that what you want?'

'It's what I want and what I demand!'

Dark eyebrows soared with disapproval. 'My, my . . . Do I detect the beginnings of a tantrum?' Then the strong jaw clenched as he leaned forward and informed her, 'I wouldn't advise such behaviour with me. It could prove highly counter-productive. You see, I'm just liable to lose my patience and drag you right out of that car to give you a lesson in how to behave.'

Camilla threw him a look of contempt. 'I doubt very much that you're qualified to give lessons in anything to anybody. And certainly not in anything relating to civilised behaviour!' But, as she said it, for safety's sake she placed her hand strategically near the door-handle, just in case he should have the temerity to attempt to keep his overbearing threat. The look in those menacing iron-grey eyes more than suggested that he might.

They bored into her like steel drills as he came back at her now, his tone taut as a whiplash as he observed, 'You appear to have an answer for everything.' Condemnation tugged at his lip. 'So I'm sure you're perfectly capable of dealing with this tiresome little problem yourself and clearing the road without my help.' With a final dark look and a contemptuous shrug, he started, elaborately, to turn away.

'Hey, there! Wait a minute! You can't just walk off and leave me here!'

Dark eyes glanced crushingly over his shoulder. 'Oh, no? Just watch me, lady!'

'But what am I supposed to do? Perhaps you expect me to sprout wings and fly?'

He paused a couple of feet away and turned with a harsh look to meet her gaze. 'I don't give a damn what you do. Sprout wings, if you like. You're damned well high and mighty enough! Just so long as you don't use your horn and frighten the sheep in the process.'

'But it's your job to control these animals, not mine! I demand that you get them out of my way!'

'*Demand*?' A dark scowl thundered across his face. 'That's a word you use rather a lot. And one, I'm very much afraid, that will get you absolutely nowhere with me.'

Camilla glared at him. To get anywhere with this savage was positively the last thing she desired. But, without his assistance, she knew she was stuck. Perhaps she ought to try a different tactic.

With a flash of inspiration, she glanced at her watch. 'The reason I'm in such a hurry,' she offered in a suddenly reasonable tone, 'is because I happen to have a very important business appointment to keep with the Laird of Glen Crannach.' She was bending the truth ever so slightly, but perhaps, since all else had apparently failed, a strategic bit of name-dropping might not go amiss.

A totally inscrutable look settled on the stranger's face as the iron-grey eyes surveyed her now. 'Do you, indeed?' he observed. 'To have an appointment with such an eminent old gentleman, you yourself must surely be a person of some considerable consequence . . .'

As he paused, Camilla looked back at him in silence, uncertain of the underlying meaning of his remark. Then she listened with irritation as, running a hand over his unruly dark hair, he continued calmly, 'However, it was my understanding that the Laird is in rather poor health these days.'

And what would a ruffian like him possibly know about such things? Determined not to concede an inch, Camilla unflinchingly met his gaze. 'I'm extremely sorry to hear it. However, should it happen to be true, I'm sure the Laird's heir and grandson, the Honourable Ross McKeown, will take care of me in his grandfather's stead.' She regarded him archly, proud of herself. With a little unwitting assistance from him, she had dropped in two names for the price of one!

'That will no doubt be the Honourable Ross McKeown's pleasure.' An amused smile flickered in the corners of the mobile, well-shaped mouth, and the iron-grey eyes seemed to pause for a moment to study her more closely, taking in every detail of the perfect oval of her face, with its soft, shiny frame of long blonde hair, perfect English rose complexion, bright blue eyes and rosebud mouth.

Then one dark eyebrow arched appreciatively as his eyes drifted insolently downwards to apply their unhurried scrutiny to the softly feminine curves of her breasts that rose and fell with growing indignation beneath the pale blue cashmere of her sweater.

How dared he examine her like that with that bold, hedonistic look on his face? Somehow, just his gaze on her had felt as intimate and real as a caress—and, treacherously, Camilla could sense her unsuspecting flesh responding, her skin growing warm and tingly all over, as he continued his scrutiny a wanton moment longer before returning his attentions once more to her face.

Yet, in spite of the indignity of that sensuous assault that Camilla was still struggling to overcome, she at least had the satisfaction of observing that her little ploy had had the desired effect. Her casual introduction into the conversation of the names of the local gentry had evidently aroused his interest—and perhaps even a bit of timely respect. She allowed herself a brief smile of satisfaction and awaited his more co-operative response.

Vain hope! The man was pathologically incapable of respect, and co-operation, most likely, was a word he had never heard. She felt her smile crumble with frustration as he came to lean arrogantly against the side of the car. Then, casually pushing back the sleeves of his sweater to reveal strong, tanned forearms, he informed her, in a tone of malicious satisfaction that belied the synthetic sympathy of his words, 'If you're headed for Castle Crannach, I'm sorry to tell you you're going the wrong way. There's a turning about five miles back along the road that you should have taken.'

'I didn't see any wretched turning!' she protested futilely, blue eyes accusing him.

He merely smiled a superior smile. 'Nevertheless, I assure you it's there.'

Camilla didn't doubt for one moment that it was. Hadn't she been missing turnings and misreading road signs right from the very outset of this ill-starred journey? It was almost beginning to feel as though she might never reach the castle at all—an eventuality which, all things considered, might not be such a terrible thing.

For the absolute truth of the matter was that Camilla had been less than overjoyed about this assignment right from the day it had landed in her lap. Maybe fate was trying to tell her now that she should just turn around and go straight back. One thing was absolutely for certain—she didn't belong in this alien place!

With a sigh of resignation—in spite of her personal misgivings, it was her duty to get on and do the job she'd come to do—she started to jam the gear-lever into reverse. 'Five miles back, you say?' she muttered bad-temperedly. 'I don't suppose you could find it in your heart to tell me which side of the road it's on?'

'You'll find it on the right-hand side. You can't really miss it. It's the only turning for miles.'

Camilla nodded doubtfully. As soon as someone

uttered those fateful words, 'you can't miss it', somehow she always did.

The iron-grey eyes were watching her as he offered, with a sarcastic smile, 'If you're really as helpless as you would have me believe, I suppose I could always draw you a map.'

Helpless? No one had ever called her that before. He was evidently as poor a judge of character as he was unpalatable as a man. She straightened and threw him a hostile look. 'That won't be necessary, thank you very much.'

He held her gaze, as though he could read her mind. 'Somehow, that's what I thought you'd say.' Then he took a step back and hooked his thumbs once more into the pockets of his body-hugging jeans. 'As I said, it's on the right-hand side of the road, just after the hump-backed bridge, on the north side of the burn.' As Camilla frowned, he clarified, 'A burn's what we call a stream in this part of the world.' He smiled an irritating smile. 'Another little word for you to add to your vocabulary.'

Camilla was far too much of a lady to offer aloud the suggestion that instantly crossed her mind as to what she would like to see him do with his contributions to her vocabulary! Instead, she smiled a tight-lipped smile as she swung the steering-wheel round to execute a neat three-point turn, and informed him caustically through the still-open window, 'Thank you for everything. It's really been most educational.'

'Don't mention it. Any time.' There was no lack of vinegar in his own reply. 'Though I would hope that next time we meet I won't be required to waste so much time instructing you on how to behave.'

Confounded upstart! Of all the nerve! 'Don't worry,' she assured him, with needles in her voice. 'I haven't the faintest intention of wasting another single second of your time!'

'Good. I'm glad to hear it.' With a dismissive swagger, he turned away. 'I would say that was an admirable intention . . . for both our sakes.'

Damned arrogance, Camilla was thinking irritably to herself as she slammed the gear-stick into second and jabbed her foot down hard on the accelerator. Yet she couldn't suppress a private, sardonic little chortle as she wound up the window and headed down the road. Next time we meet, indeed! There was never going to be a next time—at least, not if she saw him first! And if she did, she just might seriously consider mowing down his arrogant personage, along with his herd of road-blocking sheep! She bit her lip and mentally corrected herself. Flock, not herd. He'd been right about that.

To her mingled amazement and relief, she found the turning to Glen Crannach exactly where he'd said it was. Though it was hardly surprising that she'd missed it the first time . . . The crooked little signpost that announced its presence was all but completely obscured by a clump of leafy rowan trees, their fingerlike leaves a warm russet-gold in the early autumn sun.

She glanced at her watch and made a quick calculation. According to the information on the signpost, it was eight and a half miles to Glen Crannach. If she could manage this last lap of her journey without taking another wrong turning along the way, she might just make it to the castle in time for her appointment with Ross McKeown.

For she was already perfectly well aware that the old Laird himself was poorly and that all his affairs these days were being handled by his grandson, Ross. She had been informed of that much by the secretary she had spoken to when she had phoned from London to set up this job. But she had not been about to discuss such matters, which clearly were no concern of his, with that detestable individual with the sheep!

As she drove along, praying at every bend in the road that she might not encounter any more sheep, Camilla found her thoughts straying uneasily to the week that lay ahead—and wondering why it was that she felt so ambivalent about this job.

OK, so the Highlands of Scotland weren't exactly Paris or Florence. Some might say she had drawn the short straw when it had come to the handing out of jobs . . .

It was Anni who had broken the good news about the Meredith assignment. 'Guess what? They're bringing out a new series of art books and they want Focus to supply the photographs for three of them—*French Impressionism, The Italian Renaissance* and *The Celtic Heritage of Scotland*!'

Which was really quite a coup for Focus, the small but highly respected photographic studio that Anni and her partners, Camilla and Sue, ran from a corner of a converted warehouse at the back of Covent Garden. Yet Camilla had felt a pang of unease—and had known long before her name was picked out of the hat that she was the one destined to end up eating haggis for a week rather than tortellini or pâté de foie gras!

'Cheer up,' Sue had commiserated when her expectations were confirmed. 'I hear the heather's blooming at this time of year!'

It was, too. As she sped now along the rough, deserted road, the hills all around were a rich, brilliant purple, really quite breathtakingly beautiful. And, to be perfectly truthful, she didn't really care too much about missing out on France or Italy. She had visited both countries before, whereas this was her very first visit to Scotland.

Yet there was something indefinable, like some sixth sense deep in her soul, that made her feel edgy and afraid. Quite illogically, she felt threatened—as she had before she had even stepped on to the plane.

It was all to do with Eric, she suspected, and his proposal of marriage just two nights ago.

It was something she had long been expecting, and she had had her answer ready. She had been going out with Eric now for almost a year and she knew that he was precisely what she was looking for in a husband. A brilliant solicitor, at twenty-nine four years older than herself, he shared her own love of a quiet life, with just the right sprinkling of restaurant dinners and theatrical outings to keep monotony at bay. And, above all, he came from, and would provide for her, the sort of stable, secure background that throughout her turbulent childhood had been no more than an unreachable dream.

So, the other night, when he had popped the question over dinner at a West End restaurant, her unequivocal acceptance had been ready on her lips.

She had been momentarily stunned when he had held up his hand with a sympathetic smile and enjoined her, 'I know this is a very big decision and you probably need some time to consider. So, think it over while you're up in Scotland. You can give me your answer when you get back.'

She had been half-way to protesting that she didn't need time to think. But she had hesitated, and then, as he had turned to call the waiter, it had suddenly been too late. And that was more or less precisely when her feelings of anxiety had started to grow. Almost as though she feared that with that momentary hesitation she had somehow jeopardised all that was most important to her.

Of course, it was utterly ridiculous, she told herself firmly now. And equally illogical and foolish was the manner in which she had somehow transferred her personal anxieties to this trip to the Highlands. Almost as though she believed that this place would be the instrument of her downfall. It was a stupid and irrational fear. As soon as this week was over she would, quite simply, return to London and give Eric her answer, in the affirmative. Then her life would continue exactly as planned.

At that moment her attention was distracted by something approaching in her rear-view mirror. Something that appeared to be travelling at a quite remarkable speed.

As it began to gain on her, she could make out a dusty-looking Land Rover which, in wilful defiance of the narrowness of the road, was quite evidently intent on overtaking her. Lest she doubt that, its horn suddenly gave a monstrous blare, making her swerve abruptly into the side of the road as, throwing up a hail of small stones, it went roaring arrogantly past.

It had all happened too fast for her to be able to make out the driver, but she raised an angry fist at him all the same, as he and his dusty vehicle disappeared at full speed round a bend. 'Damned cowboy!' she railed indignantly. Then she paused for a moment to catch her breath, oddly shaken by the incident. It seemed to be yet another manifestation of the menace and hostility of this place. And, again, the gnawing preoccupation assailed her that perhaps it had been a mistake to come.

Impatiently she cast the thought aside. It was too late now to let her insecurities swamp her. She was here and she had a job to do—and she was jolly well going to get on with it!

She took only one wrong turning along the remainder of the road to Glen Crannach, but she was already too far behind schedule to stop off and check in at the Stag Hotel, where she was booked for the duration of her stay. She was due at the castle at four o'clock and her professional pride would not allow her to be late.

She arrived at the gates with ten minutes to spare and paused for a moment to admire the stately grey stone edifice with its parapets and towers, set back discreetly from the road amid undulating, russet-gold trees. So this was the home of the fifteenth Laird of Glen Crannach, not to mention also the home of what had brought her here—namely, the most comprehensive private collection in the world of early Celtic art.

She smiled appreciatively to herself. And a fitting

home it appeared to be. The handsome Castle Crannach was surely everyone's idea of what a Scottish castle should be! As she made her way up the gravel drive, she was happily surprised to feel a faint glow of enthusiasm for the job ahead.

The first slightly chastening blow to her suddenly lifting spirits came as she drove up to the main door of the castle. For there, parked right outside, was an exceedingly dusty Land Rover, remarkably similar in every detail to the one she had encountered just a short while ago.

But it must be another, she hastily reassured herself as she climbed out of her almost equally dusty hire car and lifted her camera-bag from the back seat. Four-wheel-drives in this part of the world were probably as common as red buses down in London. It was surely quite unthinkable that anyone connected with Castle Crannach could have the loutish manners of the driver of that car!

The second slightly chastening blow to her spirits came just after she had rung the doorbell — though it failed to occur to Camilla at the time that a third must be waiting in the wings. Life's demoralising little blows tended to come in sets of three.

The door opened, and a woman in a starched white apron appeared. 'Yes?' she enquired with a fearsome scowl that knocked the smile right off her visitor's face.

Camilla nodded politely at the thin, dour figure, determined not to be thrown by this somewhat chilling lack of welcome. 'I'm Camilla Holden. I have an appointment with Mr Ross McKeown.'

Shrewd nut-brown eyes regarded her from a pale, lined face. 'In that case, you'd better come in.'

Stiffly, the woman stood aside and allowed Camilla to step into a huge vaulted hall. Then she was leading her across a crimson carpet, emblazoned with the McKeown coat of arms, and through a double doorway into a large reception room. 'Wait here,' the woman commanded brusquely. Then, with a crackle of her starched apron, she was gone.

Alone, Camilla paused to look around her. Wow! This was really something else! Who ever said that the British landed gentry had fallen on hard times? There was definitely no evidence of poverty here! From the magnificent crystal chandeliers to the Aubusson tapestry on one wall, every antique stick of furniture and every precious ornament proclaimed wealth and lineage and taste.

Without even thinking, she was unzipping her camera-bag and fitting her Nikon with the appropriate lens. For already her sharp eyes had homed in on several of the Celtic artefacts that were dotted about the splendid room, and, like a marksman spying his prey, her finger was itching to squeeze the trigger.

Next moment she was moving about the room, clicking excitedly. This place was a treasure-trove, and she hadn't even glimpsed the real collection yet! As her spirits began to soar again, somehow she knew beyond a doubt that the heir to all these treasures, the man she was about to meet, had to be a man after her own heart. A man of immaculate taste and finesse, who took pleasure in the cultural delicacies of life.

It was starting to look, after all, as though her trip might turn out to be a resounding success!

'So, Miss Holden, I see you've arrived!'

At the sound of a male voice, Camilla swung round, a smile of delight etched on her face. For little did she suspect that the vision that would meet her eyes represented the third and most demoralising blow of all. In an instant, the smile had frozen on her lips and her heart was plummeting to the floor.

'Surely, it can't be . . .!' she gasped in silent horror.

But there could be no doubt. It was.

With a faintly amused, superior smile, the wild-looking, dark-haired figure in the Aran sweater and body-hugging jeans stepped towards her and extended his hand. 'So, we meet again. I'm the Honourable Ross McKeown.'

CHAPTER TWO

CAMILLA gaped at him as he came towards her. This was surely the sickest joke that fate could possibly have chosen to play on her.

Cool, strong fingers gripped hers briefly. Then, holding her gaze, Ross McKeown smiled, evidently appreciating the joke more than she. 'So, you made it, after all. I take it, then, that you didn't run into any more "herds" of sheep?'

Camilla straightened to her full five foot seven, but she still felt only about two inches tall. With accusing blue eyes she looked up into his face, a good six or seven inches higher than her own. 'Why didn't you tell me who you were?'

'I don't seem to remember you asking.' A hard look replaced the humour in his eyes, silently reminding her of the imperious manner in which she had assumed him to be a lowly farm worker when they had last met, just over an hour ago. 'You were so busy trying to lay down the law that my identity was the least of your concerns.'

Inwardly Camilla winced. She couldn't deny that the accusation was true. And, though she was far from proud of the way she had acted, the very notion of apologising stuck in her craw. After all, his own behaviour had not exactly been worthy of applause.

'But you knew who I was, didn't you?' she charged.

'Not immediately, but I guessed soon enough.

Somehow your overbearing manner fitted precisely with my image of a big-city photographer.'

That was an uncomfortable gibe—as much a slur on her profession as it was on her. 'I was lost,' she protested weakly, offering what sounded like a serviceable excuse. And feeling grouchy and frustrated and tired, she might have added.

But she was glad she hadn't as Ross rebuked her impatiently, 'Spare me a repeat of the helpless act, Miss Holden. You, I would suggest, are about as helpless as a she-cat with six sets of claws. And if there's one breed on this planet I have absolutely no time for, it's conniving, manipulative women!'

Camilla paled at the insult and was momentarily lost for a suitable response. Earlier she had taken him for a poor judge of character. Now he was just being downright rude. Perhaps, it occurred to her, as with an effort she met the iron-hard gaze, she had given mortal offence by assuming him to be a humble shepherd.

She swallowed on the lump in her throat, acutely, claustrophobically conscious now of the ferocious aura of male power that radiated out of him. Every hard-packed sinew of that muscular body, every domineering line in his granite-hewn face somehow seemed to menace her with its aggressive affirmation of authority and strength. She wished he weren't standing quite so close as she told him now, defensively, 'It was perfectly natural for me to assume that those sheep were yours.'

One eyebrow lifted. 'Indeed, the sheep *are* mine, Miss Holden.' Then he smiled a humourless smile as he added, 'However, it was quite by chance that I happened to be there with them. Just a couple of minutes before you came blundering on to the scene, I was passing, on my way home. I stopped to give old Jock, one of our shepherds, a hand with a ewe that had wandered off and got tangled up in some bushes in the woods. We'd just about got her free when you almost scattered the entire flock with that infernal blaring horn of yours.'

Suddenly Camilla couldn't resist it. 'You're pretty handy with the horn yourself.' She now knew exactly who the cowboy in the Land Rover had been!

Ross allowed himself a fleeting smile, revealing very even, very white teeth. 'I was out to give you a fright. You were driving much too fast.'

'Then so were you.' She narrowed her eyes at him as he led her now across the room to a group of sofas and bade her sit, noting with a *frisson* of displeasure how he carelessly stretched his legs out in front of him, as he sank down into the sofa opposite, so that the brown leather shoes he wore were only inches away from her own.

As she laid down her camera on the coffee-table between them, she adjusted her blue skirt over her knees and pointedly moved her feet to one side. 'I seem to remember you overtaking me without any trouble at all.'

'That's different.'

Camilla barely suppressed an ironical snort. 'Yes, somehow I thought it might be!'

Ross McKeown held her eyes for a moment, causing her to drop her gaze. Then, very carefully, he elaborated, 'It's different because I know the road. And, since the seats in a Land Rover are considerably higher off the ground than they are in a car like yours. I had the additional advantage of a far superior view of the road.' He leaned magisterially against the cushions as the iron-grey eyes raked her face. '*I'd* have been able to stop in time if I'd come upon a flock of sheep.'

Camilla flushed and glanced up at him again. 'I stopped in time!' she defended.

He held her eyes. 'But only just. I seem to remember you came within a hair's breadth of ploughing straight into the whole damned lot.' He paused for a moment, then added pointedly, 'And in these parts, the irresponsible killing of sheep is considered to be a serious offence!'

'I suppose you hold public executions—with hanging, drawing and quartering, and popcorn for the onlookers at half-time?'

Her sarcasm was not lost on him, but Ross McKeown did not smile. 'Not for killing sheep, Miss Holden. We reserve our more spectacular punishments for more socially objectionable crimes. Like pig-headed arrogance and overbearing conceit.'

In spite of a sharp stab of irritation, Camilla laughed out loud at that. That *he*, of all people, should accuse *her*! 'In that case, I'm very much surprised that you're still around to tell the tale!'

At that moment, they were interrupted as the woman in the white starched apron appeared through the doorway, pushing a trolley. So, it was teatime at Castle Crannach. And at the tantalising aroma of hot, buttered pancakes, fluffy fruit scones and Highland oatmeal bannocks, Camilla was suddenly very much aware of just how long it was since she'd last eaten.

'Thank you, Maggie. I'll do the honours.' As the woman arranged the tea things on the heavy mahogany coffee-table, Ross gestured politely to her to leave. Then, with the dour-faced Maggie gone, he set about adroitly pouring tea from a fine Meissen teapot into fragile Meissen cups.

Camilla watched him with a strange fascination. There was something both incongruous and faintly appealing about the vision presented by this ultra-masculine man, with his wild, dark hair and ferocious grey eyes, as he handled the delicate gold-leafed porcelain. For, in spite of his powerful, broad dimensions, the well-shaped hands had a sensitive touch. They seemed to move with feather-light precision as, with the minimum of fuss, they accomplished their task.

He leaned towards her, extending a cup. 'Your tea, Miss Holden. Help yourself to sugar and something to eat.' And as for a moment his gaze meshed with hers and his hand came within a thread's breadth of her own, Camilla caught a flash of something oddly intimate and deeply unsettling in his eyes. Something totally unexpected. Something she could not properly decipher, nor even begin to identify. Yet it sent a sudden chill through her bones and a stab of sharp panic skittering in her heart.

For, in some strange and inexplicable way, what she had seemed to glimpse in that moment of revelation was the real and terrifying dark substance of the nagging apprehension that had been preying on her for days.

Ross brought her back to earth with a bump. 'I think it's time we got down to discussing the reason why you're here.' He leaned back in his seat again and surveyed her with penetrating, cool grey eyes. 'You haven't come all this distance, after all, just to sample our Highland hospitality.'

Indeed she had not. She laid down her cup. 'I've come to photograph the Celtic collection for this new art series that Meredith's is bringing out.' A sudden furrow marred her brow as an anxious thought occurred to her. 'I made all the arrangements through your secretary. I presume they have your approval?' It would be disastrous, she was thinking, if he were to veto the project now. And, having glimpsed the perverse, impulsive nature of the man, she could not safely rule out that possibility.

'The collection has been photographed before. Could not Meredith's have used photographs from those previous sources?'

Politely, Camilla shook her head. 'The whole series is to be put together with new and original photographs. They're looking for a totally fresh approach. They're not using any old source material at all.' Hence her partners' parallel trips to Paris and Florence. And I'll bet the Louvre and the Uffizi aren't giving them half the hassle that I'm being given here! she thought sourly. She forced a smile and added equably, 'In the field of fine arts publication, Meredith's is very highly regarded. Naturally, they wish to preserve that reputation. They want only to produce the best.'

'Which is why, I presume, they're hiring you?'

Camilla stiffened, resenting the taunt. He had managed to make the observation a blanket disapprobation of Meredith's judgement. 'They hired us because they believed we would do the job well. Our studio has done work for them before.'

'Yes, you did the *Stately Homes of England* collection and another on Victorian bric-à-brac.'

Camilla's eyes widened in frank astonishment. So he had taken the trouble to dig into her credentials. Then her astonishment doubled as he continued, 'And a very fine job you did of them, too. Which is why you have my full permission to go ahead with the job you've come to do. You may be lacking in other qualities'—the iron-grey eyes held hers disparagingly—'but you appear to be an able photographer.'

So she had misinterpreted that earlier taunt. His disapproval of her appeared to be directed at her personal, not her professional qualities. Well and good. Ross McKeown's judgement of her on a personal level mattered to her not one jot. After all, it could scarcely be any lower than her own scathing personal judgement of him. As long as she had his professional respect, she required nothing more of him.

'Perhaps, once we've finished here'—he pushed the plate of scones towards her as she reached out for a second one—'I can very quickly show you the collection and you can start thinking about how you want to set it up?' He leaned back in his seat again and rubbed long, strong fingers over his chin as he went on to put to her, with a faintly curious lift of one eyebrow, 'I take it you'll be wanting to shoot the *Ceò do dh'òr* as well?'

Camilla frowned.

'The Golden Mist. *Ceò do dh'òr* is its Gaelic name.' And it sounded even more beautiful in Gaelic than in English. She nodded affirmatively. 'Oh, yes. Definitely.' The legendary set of jewels that were said to have belonged to Scotland's Queen Margaret were her top priority on this assignment. 'I want to do something really special with them.'

A smile of challenge flickered across his lips. 'I take it, then, that you're not afraid of the curse?'

Camilla swallowed and took a deep breath. Inclined to be slightly superstitious by nature, she had to confess that the story of the *Ceò do dh'òr* curse had sent a shiver down her spine when first she'd heard it. But she looked boldly across at Ross McKeown now. 'Why should *I* be afraid of the curse? *You're* the one who should be afraid. I understand it affects only the heirs of the Lairds of Glen Crannach.'

'So they say.' Ross seemed totally unperturbed, even scathingly amused, as he continued to enlighten her, 'The jewels were a gift from King David to an ancient ancestor of mine at a time when the McKeowns' seat of power was centred on the Isle of Mhoire. It was only at the end of the eighteenth century that my family moved their base to Glen Crannach—bringing the *Ceò do dh'òr* jewels with them, of course. The jewels have never left McKeown hands.'

He paused a moment before continuing, observing Camilla's rapt expression. 'However, over the two hundred years since the jewels were moved, three of my ancestors have met sudden and somewhat mysterious deaths. My father, his grandfather, and his grandfather before him. All were in their thirty-fifth year and all were the current heirs at the time. According to the legend, you see, the jewels must never leave the Isle of Mhoire.'

'So why do you keep them here?' It was no more than idle curiosity that made her ask. If the headstrong Ross McKeown wished to tempt fate by flying in the teeth of an ancient Celtic curse, that was entirely up to him. 'Wouldn't it be more sensible to keep them on the island? For the sake of preserving your family's title, at least? After all, you are the last in line.' To her knowledge, the unmarried Ross had a sister, but the title was not permitted to pass to a woman.

'I appreciate your concern.' His tone was mocking as he met her eyes. 'But I'm afraid I don't share it. I don't happen to believe in curses, you see. I believe in things that can be substantiated by the laws of science and good sense. The accidents that happened to my father and the others are all capable of logical explanation, I'm sure. The coincidence of their ages, along with the fact that they all happened to be the current heir at the time, I can assure you, is no more than that—a somewhat bizarre, but totally meaningless coincidence.

'But we shall see . . .' He shrugged and paused to run long, tanned fingers slowly through his thick dark hair. 'I still have a couple of months to go until my thirty-fifth birthday . . .' He smiled a wry smile, still watching her. 'If I can survive till the end of November unscathed, then the curse will be revealed for the hokum it is.'

Hokum, he blandly called it, and it might well be. But Camilla knew for certain that she herself would never have taken such a risk, and she found herself marvelling slightly at the self-assurance of the man. Though in her mind she instantly dismissed that self-assurance for the unutterable arrogance it really was. Ross McKeown quite clearly believed that he possessed powers beyond those of ordinary mortals!

Cynically, she observed aloud, 'Just so long as you manage to survive till the end of this week, when I've finished my pictures. It would really be most inconvenient if you were to drop dead half-way through the shoot.'

He smiled crookedly, seeming to appreciate this dark humour. 'Then I shall try my very best not to inconvenience you.' He laid down his cup and started to stand up. 'Perhaps, if you've had enough to eat, we can go through and have a look at the collection?'

Without any difficulty at all, Camilla could have polished off the remaining pancakes, bannocks and scones. If they were the work of the dour-faced Maggie, then the woman's skill as a cook more than made up for her lack of charm. But Ross was evidently eager to make a move, so she laid aside her napkin and got to her feet. 'I'm ready,' she assured him. Then she grabbed her camera and slung it over her shoulder as, without preamble, he headed for the door.

He led her out into the hall, then along a corridor and up a short flight of stairs, till they came to a heavy, oak-panelled door. Then he reached into the pocket of his jeans and drew out an elaborate-looking key. 'This whole room is specially protected,' he told her as he turned the key in the lock. 'And the only person who knows where the key is kept, aside from my grandfather and myself, is Maggie.' He pushed the door open and stood aside to let Camilla pass. 'Please. Go ahead.'

Camilla gasped at the sight that met her eyes. She had already seen and closely studied most of the previous photographs of the collection, but none of them had done anything like justice to the staggering beauty of the real thing.

'I can't believe it! There's so much more here than I'd expected, and it's all so beautiful!'

In delighted admiration, she glanced round at the displays of ancient artefacts, from silver *quaichs,* or drinking bowls, to bejewelled horn snuff mulls and stone-carved Celtic crosses, her brain already racing with ideas on how best to make them come alive on film. She grinned at Ross. 'It's magnificent! I can't wait to get started!' Then, her excitement bubbling, 'Where's the *Ceò do dh'òr?*'

'In here.' He was crossing to a steel-clad wall safe and quickly keying in the combination. 'Normally, it's kept in here,' he advised her. 'But just for this week, while you're doing the photographs, we'll leave it in one of the cabinets with the other bits of jewellery.'

As he spoke, he withdrew from the safe a carved wooden box with a silver lock and key. Then, laying the box on a nearby table, he turned the key and raised the lid.

'The *Ceò do dh'òr.*' He stood aside to let her see and smiled at the wonder that lit up her eyes. 'The jewels of a queen and saint. Nearly a thousand years old.'

On a soft bed of dark blue velvet lay an exquisite set of matching necklace, bracelet and ring, fashioned from ancient silver and studded with semi-precious gems. With admiring eyes, Camilla gazed at it. 'It's hard to believe it's really that old.'

'You like it?'

'*Like* it? It's a work of art!'

'Here. Take a closer look.' With strong, delicate fingers Ross lifted the bracelet from the box and handed it to her. 'Try it on. See how it feels.'

Nervously, Camilla slipped it over her wrist. It felt regal and heavy and precious and cool.

'It suits you.' As she glanced up to meet his eyes, he reached for the necklace and held it up and, though she guessed instantly what he was about to do, she didn't have the wit to step away.

The next moment he had caught her lightly by the shoulder as he held the necklace up to her throat, his fingers brushing the blonde hair aside as they reached behind to fasten the clasp.

The response that shot through her was really quite unwarranted, yet utterly, totally overpowering all the same. The touch of his fingers against the skin of her neck was like a branding iron burning into her flesh, and the brush of the broad chest against her breasts as, for a moment, the powerful arms embraced her sent shivers of pure, exquisite anguish ricocheting through her veins.

Like a drowning woman, she gulped for air as his lips seemed to come within a whisper of her cheek. She could feel the warmth of his breath against her skin and smell his clean, cool, masculine scent. Then she shuddered and swallowed drily, feeling her whole body go as limp as a rag as with delicate, sensuous fingers he paused to adjust the heavy pendant as it fell against the cleavage of her cashmere-clad breasts.

He stepped back, letting his hands slide slowly down her arms as he released her, sending goosebumps right to the soles of her feet. 'Here. See how you look.' With one hand still burning on her elbow, he proceeded to propel her across the room to where an enormous gilt-framed mirror hung against the bare stone wall. 'As you can see, they look even better on a woman than they did in the box.'

Undoubtedly she would have agreed, if she had been able to focus her attention on the jewels. But all Camilla was aware of at that moment was the tall, dark, wild-looking man at her side and his reflection looking back at her through the glass.

'Yes,' she murmured foolishly, wondering what madness this was that possessed her. And wondering, too, with helpless indignation, if he could sense the cruel havoc he had wreaked in her soul.

That thought was suddenly enough to return a measure of free will to her limbs. She turned away abruptly, fumbling to undo the clasp of the necklace before he could make a move to help her. With a stiff smile she handed it to him, taking care to make no contact with his hand. Then she slid the bracelet quickly from her wrist and handed that to him as well.

'I think I would like to photograph these outdoors, in natural light,' she told him, turning away and feeling slightly amazed at the remarkable steadiness of her own voice. 'But I'll have to look around for a suitable background. Would you be agreeable to that?'

She heard him return the pieces to the box, close

the lid, then turn the key. 'Of course. Though, naturally, if you plan to take them out of this room, I must insist on you being accompanied—either by myself or, if I'm not available, by prior arrangement, by Maggie, our housekeeper.' As she turned to glance at him with a measure of surprise, he assured her with a solemn smile, 'Maggie has been with us for years. I would trust her with my life.'

A rare and glowing commendation indeed. Somehow, Camilla did not see the Honourable Ross McKeown as a man who would lightly trust anybody with anything of his—least of all his life.

She watched as he locked the *Ceò do dh'òr* box inside one of the cabinets that lined the wall. 'I'd like to make a start tomorrow morning, as early as possible, while the light's at its best.'

'Whenever you like. I'll be up at six.'

A little earlier than she'd had in mind! 'Say about eight o'clock? I'd like to have some breakfast first.'

He shrugged as he led her towards the door. 'Eight's fine. I'll be here.'

Out in the passageway, she waited while he relocked the heavy oak-panelled door and returned the key to the pocket of his jeans. Then they made their way in single file back down the stairs and along the corridor to the hallway.

'Feel free to have a look around the grounds for locations before you leave.' Ross had paused by the reception-room doorway, leaning casually against the door-jamb as he issued the invitation.

But it was getting late. Camilla glanced quickly at her watch. 'It's time I checked in at my hotel. I'm expecting a phone call in about half an hour.'

She should not have added that extra bit of

information. She had no call to explain her private affairs to him, and she knew the minute the words left her mouth that he would pounce on them. A caustic smile curled round his lips and one dark eyebrow lifted insolently. 'Boyfriend phoning up to check that you've survived your first day in this heathen land?'

He was absolutely right, as it happened. The call she was expecting was from Eric. She threw him a cool look. 'Something like that.'

The broad shoulders beneath the Aran sweater flexed as he folded his arms across his chest, and a look of amusement flickered in his face. 'So, you have a steady boyfriend, do you?' As she disdained to answer, he leaned back his head and let his smile broaden as his eyes swept over her, impudently, openly assessing her, as though she were a piece of livestock. 'Tell me about this boyfriend of yours. No, wait a minute. Let me guess . . .'

Camilla glared a warning at him. 'Kindly don't trouble yourself. Eric is none of your damned business!'

'Eric?' He ignored her admonition and seemed to consider the name for a moment. 'I'll bet I can tell you more or less exactly what this Eric of yours is like.'

He treated her to another impertinent sweep of his dark eyes, making her flesh burn and her blood boil in a total confusion of responses. 'I'll bet he's a banker, or an accountant—or a solicitor,' he challenged. 'Someone with clean fingernails and perfect manners and not a single nasty habit to his name.'

Camilla suddenly hated Ross McKeown with an

intensity that was almost pleasurable. 'And what's wrong with clean fingernails and good manners?' she fumed. 'What's wrong with being a solicitor?'

'So, I was right?' He grinned down at her with evil enjoyment. 'I'll bet he listens to Mozart and country music and takes two weeks' summer holiday every July. His favourite food is Indian and he drinks Scandinavian beer and German wine.'

As he paused, Camilla was trembling with fury. He had reeled off his list like a damning indictment, as though passing down judgement from some superior height. And though his attitude in itself was quite maddening enough, the thing that infuriated her most of all was the fact that he had, more or less, been right.

'Have you finished?' she demanded.

'Not if you'd like me to continue. I bet I could even tell you what car he drives, not to mention the colour of his socks.'

Camilla clenched her jaw at him and resisted the urge to take a swipe. Any form of physical contact with him was something she was keen to avoid. Just being within the same four walls was already quite unpleasant enough!

'I think you must be the most contemptible, ill-mannered man I've ever had the misfortune to meet!' As the words came out in a heartfelt snarl, she noted with some satisfaction that the look of amusement had gone from his face. 'And now, if you'll excuse me . . .' Abruptly she started to push past him, intending to continue through the doorway and into the reception-room beyond. 'I left my camera-bag in there. I'll just collect it and then I'll leave.'

'Just one minute, if you don't mind!'

Before she could take evasive action, he had reached out and grabbed hold of her by one arm, sending a welter of panic-stricken questions scattering like ninepins through her brain. What vile intention was in his mind? she was wondering wildly as, roughly, he jerked her towards him so that her body crushed up against his. What ghastly, evil imposition was he planning to inflict? And suddenly all her instincts for survival were hurtling to her aid. Whatever iniquity he intended, she would put up a damned good fight!

She was totally unprepared, however, for his next unchivalrous move.

'Just one thing before you go.' In one deft movement he had snatched the camera-strap from her shoulder, releasing her abruptly at the same time, so that she staggered slightly as she fell back and could only watch in impotent horror as he snapped open the back of her precious Nikon and deftly removed the roll of film.

'What the hell do you think you're doing? I've already shot most of that!'

'Precisely.' Eyes like meat cleavers slashed her face as, very deliberately now, he proceeded to expose the entire length of film. 'No one takes photographs in my house without first receiving my permission. Don't talk to me about manners, Miss Holden, until you've acquired a few yourself.'

Camilla could have kicked herself for her earlier rash breach of protocol. Taking photographs without prior permission was not her usual mode of operation at all. But though it was undoubtedly within Ross's rights to lodge a civilised complaint, the action he had just taken had been high-handed in the extreme. 'You had no right to do that!' she seethed. 'Only part of that film was shot in your house. The rest were views I took from the road while I was driving over here.'

He was unrepentant. 'Then you'll just have to go back and take them again.'

She balled her fists and glared at him, trembling with rage at his bare-faced arrogance. 'All you had to do was *ask*, you know, and I wouldn't have used the ones of the house. But I suppose you're quite unfamiliar with such civilised procedures!'

'I suppose I am, Miss Holden.' His jaw darkened dangerously as he scowled back at her. 'But then I'm not in the habit of *asking* for my rights. I prefer to *take* them!' He thrust the camera back at her, along with the useless roll of film. 'I would advise you to bear that in mind in all your future dealings with me.'

Rigid with fury and outrage, Camilla stalked past him into the room. She was certain now beyond a shred of doubt that this assignment was destined to be a scourge on her soul.

With trembling fingers she proceeded to load the camera into the camera-bag, yank the zipper closed and hoist the heavy strap impatiently over her shoulder. Then, without even glancing in his direction as he led her across the hall to the front door, she bade him a curt and thankful, 'Goodbye.'

'So long, Miss Holden,' he answered calmly. 'Till tomorrow morning at eight.'

She was aware of him standing watching her as she made her way, stiff-legged, to the car. And though nothing in the world could have induced her to turn round and meet that odious dark gaze, she could picture with no difficulty at all the superior, triumphant smile on his face.

She climbed into her car and slammed the door shut. Damn him and all he stood for! Then, as she jabbed the key in the ignition, she paused to glance in the rear-view mirror at the tall, dark-haired figure on the castle steps and smiled maliciously to herself as a sudden comforting thought crossed her mind.

If ever there was a man who thoroughly deserved to have an ancient Celtic curse dangling over his head, that man was surely Ross McKeown!

CHAPTER THREE

CHECKING into the Stag Hotel, with its atmos-
phere of peaceful, olde-worlde charm, felt like
dropping anchor in a sleepy lagoon after a
dangerous passage on a storm-tossed sea.

With immense relief, Camilla unpacked her bags,
showered quickly and ordered some tea.
Emotionally and physically she felt exhausted, as
though she'd just gone ten rounds in a heavyweight
fight. She leaned back on the pillows of the big, soft
bed and grimaced wryly to herself. I guess I'm just
not used to coping with all these traumas any more,
she thought.

The phone on the bedside table rang—and, just
for a millisecond, Camilla paused. It was unlikely
to be Ross McKeown, but the possibility was always
there. After all, the Stag Hotel was the only hostelry
in Glen Crannach, so he was bound to have guessed
she'd be staying there. And it was most assuredly
not beyond his devilish powers to find some excuse
to bother her!

Mentally crossing her fingers, she reached out
and lifted the receiver. 'Hello?' Her tone was
cautious as she waited for the caller to reply.

'Camilla, darling! How are you, my love?'

Instant warm relief surged through her. 'Eric, it's
so good to hear you!' With a happy smile she settled
back, all her tension vanishing like magic at the
familiar, reassuring sound of his voice. 'I'm fine,'

she told him brightly. 'Just a little tired, that's all.'

'No problems, then?' he wanted to know. 'The journey and everything went smoothly, I take it?'

'Absolutely. Without a hitch.' It was a gross distortion of the truth, but there was really no need for Eric to be aware of all the hassles she had encountered today. As it was, she already felt that he sometimes worried too much about her.

'This chap, McKeown, the Laird's grandson— he's looking after you properly, is he?'

Camilla took a deep breath and sighed. If only poor Eric knew the truth! 'He briefly showed me the collection,' she answered, adroitly avoiding his question, 'and it's even more spectacular than I'd expected. This looks like turning into one of the most challenging jobs I've ever done.' And for more reasons than one! she added wryly to herself. 'But how about you?' she intervened hurriedly, before Eric could ask her any more questions. 'What have you been up to today?'

She didn't really need to ask. Today was Friday, the day Eric always made a point of snatching a quick game of squash in his lunch hour—an activity which invariably led to a recuperative evening in front of the box! Still, she listened affectionately as he recounted the minor events of his day, feeling the warm, secure mantle of his love draw round her as he ended, 'I miss you, my love.'

'I miss you, too.' And she meant it. She missed his calmness, his stability, the safe way he made her feel. 'But it won't be long,' she told him, as much to reassure herself as him. 'I'll be back before you know it.'

He blew her a kiss down the line. 'I'll call you

again,' he promised. 'Just look after yourself in the meantime—and remember to keep thinking about your answer to that question I asked you the other night.'

Camilla sighed happily as she laid down the phone. Dear Eric. If he'd insisted, he could have had his answer right there and then. For if there was one thing in the world she had no doubts about, it was that she intended to accept his proposal.

She rose from the bed and paused for a moment to gaze wistfully at her reflection in the wardrobe mirror. The china-blue eyes, so assured in public, could still, in private, appear so vulnerable that she found herself wondering how she ever managed to fool anyone at all. Couldn't the world see the frightened little girl behind the determined set of that soft, fragile mouth? She smiled to herself. Apparently not. But then the mask of self-assurance that she used for protection was just one of her many achievements over the past six years.

Since childhood, life had not been easy for Camilla. Orphaned at the age of seven, she had spent her most tender years being passed from hand to hand like a parcel between the cold comfort of a South London children's home and the intermittent warm oases of temporary foster families.

By the time she had reached eighteen, and independence, she had begun to feel like a piece of flotsam. And from that moment her overriding ambition had been to put down roots of her own.

After scrimping and scraping to put herself through college, she had proceeded to scrimp and scrape some more, till she finally managed to save enough for the deposit on a modest little flat of her own. Those had been the first steps towards her goal. Setting up Focus with Anni and Sue three years ago had been the next. And the blossoming of her relationship with Eric, whom she'd met at a party, quite by chance, had perhaps been the most important development of all. With Eric, she had ceased to feel alone for the first time. At last, there was someone in the world who truly loved her, and with whom lay the kind of secure, happy future that she longed for, and deserved.

And she loved Eric. How could she not love him, after all that his love had done for her?

So why was it, she wondered now, frowning critically at her reflection, that she had allowed Ross McKeown and his scathing observations to upset her so this afternoon? What could it possibly matter to her what that detestable man might think of Eric—someone, after all, whom he had never even met?

A frown settled on the perfect oval of her face. Yet, against all reason, he had succeeded in arousing her to a pitch of furious anger that she had rarely known before.

Biting her lip, she turned away. The fact was she had been acting a little oddly ever since her arrival here—driving her hire car like a demon, then taking pictures without authority. Perhaps there's something in the air, she wondered uneasily. And whatever it was, it didn't suit her. It didn't suit her the least little bit. The sooner she got back to London and Eric, the happier she would start to feel.

However, in the meantime. . . She pulled open the wardrobe door, her features set in resolute lines. Right now, she would forget about Ross McKeown, get dressed and go downstairs for dinner. Then she would treat herself to an early night, so that tomorrow morning she would be feeling fit and refreshed, and more than ready for their appointment at eight!

She might have been, if she'd remembered to book an alarm call before she climbed into bed. As it was, the hands of her watch were just leaving eight-thirty when she struggled to consciousness nine hours later.

She leapt from the sheets with a strangled yelp. Double blast and double damnation! Now she was really in the soup!

With a stab of panic, she grabbed for the phone. 'Get me Castle Crannach, please. Mr Ross McKeown.'

If she could apologise and let him know she was on her way, perhaps the situation could still be saved. But the secretary who answered informed her, 'I'm sorry, Mr McKeown's line is engaged.'

'Then would you give him a message, please? Tell him that Miss Holden has unfortunately been delayed, but that she'll be with him in half an hour.'

There was no time for any breakfast, just a lightning shower before she threw on some clothes—a pair of natty jodhpur-style trousers and a bottle-green crew-neck sweater. Then she tied her blonde hair back in a green ribbon, grabbed her camera-bag and went hurtling down the stairs.

It was three minutes before nine when Camilla arrived, breathless and anxious, at the castle's main door. The dusty Land Rover, she was relieved to see, was standing parked just a few feet away. So at least he had had the patience to wait.

With a squeeze of trepidation, she rang the bell and a moment later Maggie appeared. 'Good morning.' She smiled nervously into the unsmiling face. 'Mr Ross McKeown's expecting me.'

Silently, Maggie shook her head. 'Mr Ross has just gone out.'

'But——' Camilla gestured towards the dusty car as she started to protest. Then she broke off with a defeated sigh. Of course, Ross McKeown would have more than one car, and she had been a fool to imagine that he might have had the courtesy to wait for her. 'When do you expect him back?' she asked.

'I'm afraid he didn't say. He could be gone for quite some time.'

Camilla felt her spirits sink. Somehow, she had the feeling he would be. 'However,' the woman continued, 'you're welcome to come in and wait for him.' She held the door open and stood aside, but Camilla declined, shaking her head.

'If you don't mind, I'll wait out here. I'd like to have a look round the grounds.' There was no point in just sitting around uselessly indoors. She could use the time getting to know the place and looking for locations for her shots.

'Suit yourself.' Maggie gave an indifferent shrug and, a moment later, the big door closed.

Camilla left her camera-bag in the car and slung her Nikon over her shoulder. It was a pleasant enough day for a wander, she decided. A low autumn sun was shining down warmly from a near-cloudless sky.

She didn't wander too far, just in case Ross might return. But she needn't have concerned herself. More than an hour later, there was still no sign of him. In that time, however, she had spotted a couple of useful-looking locations—a lovely old sundial and a pretty gazebo—and had managed to fall into conversation with an old man in a battered felt hat who was skilfully pruning the rhododendrons.

'If you're looking for something special to photograph,' he advised her as he clipped away, 'take a trip over to Loch Maree. There's some of the bonniest scenery in the world over there.'

'Then I will.' Camilla made a mental note. It was her intention, while she was in the Highlands, to take some scenic photographs for her portfolio. As she spoke, she glanced impatiently at her watch. It was nearly half-past ten. What the devil did Ross McKeown think he was playing at?

At that very moment the air was rent by a roar like Satan escaping from the underworld. The old man turned to glance at Camilla. 'That'll be him now,' he said.

He was absolutely right. As Camilla hurried up the stone steps from the garden into the forecourt of the castle, a massive BMW motorbike came thundering up the drive with, astride it, a powerful figure in jeans and black leather who could be only one person—Ross.

As the huge machine growled to a halt, he pulled off his crash helmet and shook his dark hair. Then, still astride the great metal beast, he cast a leisurely glance at her. 'So you finally got here,' he observed.

Camilla felt a sharp surge of anger. 'I've been here since before nine o'clock!' she shot back at him from between clenched teeth.

'Is that a fact?' With an air of total lack of concern, he pulled the black leather gauntlets from his hands. 'I must have just missed you, then. I went out just after half-eight.'

More or less immediately after her phone call, Camilla deduced without too much difficulty. He had quite evidently made a point of absenting himself before she had had time to arrive. But she knew better than to voice the accusation. He had deliberately kept her waiting, but she was the one who had missed their appointment—and she could read all too clearly the unspoken challenge that was written in his eyes. One word of complaint from her and he would demolish her!

His tone was deceptively mild, however, as he loosened the zipper of his black leather jerkin and subjected her to that iron-grey gaze. 'Too bad you got held up and couldn't make it for eight o'clock.' In one fluid movement, he had dismounted and propped the huge bike up on its stand, as smoothly and effortlessly as though it weighed nothing at all. 'I guess it must have been pretty tedious for you, having to hang around here with nothing to do?'

'No, not in the least,' she lied. That he had kept her waiting for so long was already quite galling enough. She would not give him the added satisfaction of knowing that his ill-mannered gesture had riled her quite as severely as he had intended that it should. 'I took the liberty of looking around,' she told him, boldly meeting his gaze. 'And I also had an extremely pleasant little chat with your gardener.'

One dark eyebrow lifted interrogatively. 'My gardener?' he enquired.

'Your gardener,' Camilla affirmed with impatience. What was the matter, didn't he know he had one? 'He very kindly suggested some places I might go to take some scenic pictures.'

Ross smiled, the superior and faintly irritating smile of one enjoying a private joke. 'He knows the area very well,' he observed. 'I'm sure he gave you good advice.'

Camilla watched as he laid his gauntlets and helmet on the saddle of the bike, feeling oddly unsettled by the powerful dark presence. The black leather jerkin, with its heavy stitching and metal-toothed zippers, seemed to emphasise and add a flavour of menace to the already broad lines of his commanding physique. Even the innocent blue jeans seemed to cling more threateningly to his muscular thighs, moulding every swell and contour, shamelessly seducing her virginal eye.

'So, what do you have in mind right now?'

With a start, she raised her eyes to his. 'What do you mean?' she asked, momentarily thrown.

'I thought you'd come here to take some photographs. Do you want to take them or not?'

'Of course that's what I came for . . .' Self-consciously, she cleared her throat and folded her arms across her chest. 'But I haven't figured out yet how I want to shoot them.' She fixed her eyes on the granite-carved face with its mocking dark eyes and wide, passionate mouth and made an effort to marshal her thoughts. 'I need to go back and have a closer look at the collection, and I'd like to do a couple of Polaroids, just as a preliminary.'

'What about locations? Have you got those sorted out?'

'A couple.' So many questions! 'Why?' she enquired, an edge to her voice.

'Well, it's just a thought . . .' he ran one hand thoughtfully over his hair ' . . . but you said you wanted to do something special with the *Ceò do dh'òr*, and last night it occurred to me that maybe I know just the place for the sort of thing you have in mind.'

Camilla dropped her arms from her chest and stuffed her hands into the pockets of her trousers. Somehow, she doubted very much that he had even the remotest idea of what it was she had in mind. She raised one sceptical eyebrow at him. 'Oh?' she enquired without enthusiasm.

He held her eyes. 'Would you like me to show you?'

She shrugged. 'OK. Why not?' It would almost certainly be a waste of time, but it would be a little ungracious for her to refuse.

He smiled, revealing those very white teeth. 'Let's go, then. Follow me.'

She found herself being led round to the back of the castle, then, as they departed from the gravel path, across rougher ground, between some trees. And in order to keep up with him Camilla virtually had to run, tripping and stumbling from time to time as her foot caught on some rock or fallen branch. 'What is this—some kind of route march?' she enquired crossly to his broad back.

He tossed her an unsympathetic glance over his leather-clad shoulder. 'Don't worry, we're almost there. Just another couple of yards to go.'

More like a couple of hundred! Camilla thought indignantly, as at last they came to an unprepossessing ruin, half-covered with climbing ivies and moss. 'Is this it?' she demanded irritably, casting a discreet but dismayed glance downwards at her scuffed and mud-spattered Gucci shoes.

Ross followed her gaze. 'If I'd known you were wearing designer footwear I'd have offered to carry you,' he caustically observed.

'An offer, I can assure you, I would have refused.' Better to sacrifice a dozen pairs of Guccis than to surrender herself to such a fate! She glanced past him, critically. 'So, what's this place supposed to be?'

'It's the old chapel of St Margaret. Or it used to be. It was deconsecrated last century—and, as you can see, it's fallen somewhat into a state of disrepair.'

Indeed. And a highly unlikely setting it looked for the shooting of the *Ceò do dh'òr*!

Ross appeared to read her mind. 'What I want to show you is inside. Down in the crypt,' he added, as she frowned. He turned away, through the tangle of weeds. 'Follow me. And watch your feet.'

Camilla could feel her impatience growing. She'd already had enough of this wild-goose chase, and now he was planning to entice her down into the dark and damp bowels of the earth! Perhaps it was his idea of a joke, or perhaps he was simply out to rile her. Probably the latter, she decided as, once inside the ruined chapel walls, he proceeded to escort her down a set of winding, rough-hewn stairs. It was his way of putting in her place what he perceived as a soft and snobbish southerner.

As they left the daylight behind, they were suddenly plunged into semi-darkness. She heard his footsteps pause. 'Here. Perhaps you'd better take my hand.' And the next moment he reached out and she felt his warm skin brush her fingers.

Instantly she snatched them away. 'Thank you, but I'll manage!' she assured him shrilly, not liking in the least the strange way her blood had leapt at his touch.

'OK. Suit yourself.' He turned away and hurried ahead of her, as she continued to grope her way behind him, praying with every shred of her being that she wouldn't lose her footing and fall. A twisted ankle was the least she feared. She feared much more making a clumsy fool of herself!

But, suddenly, as they came round the final corkscrew bend, the darkness fled and she could see again. Ross was standing at the foot of the stairs. 'Congratulations. You made it,' he said.

So sorry to disappoint you, she told him silently with her eyes. Wouldn't he just have loved to see her go sprawling, camera, Gucci shoes and all!

His footsteps echoed in the cool, dank air of the ancient, vaulted crypt as he led her through a maze of archways to a corner overlooked by a high, unglazed window. Shafts of multicoloured sunlight spilled through it on to the jagged-hewn walls. He said, turning to look at her, 'This is the place I was thinking of as a backdrop for the *Ceò do dh'òr.*'

Camilla narrowed her eyes and gazed round. 'I see,' she said, her tone non-committal.

'The light is particularly good early in the morning. It illuminates the whole of this little area.'

She could see that it would, and she could also see that, for her purposes, this place was quite ideal. But she was also ungenerously loath to admit as much to Ross McKeown. He had, by some singular freak of judgement, turned up precisely what she had been after, but she was quite definitely not about to heap praise and gratitude on him!

Assuming an air of indecision, she proceeded to scrutinise the area, pausing, hands in pockets, to examine more closely the high, open window. Sunlight splashed across her head and shoulders, making her blonde hair gleam like burnished silk, softly highlighting the curve of her breasts beneath the lightly clinging sweater.

She was not aware of the iron-grey eyes that watched her with fascination, nor was she prepared for the abrupt shift of direction in the conversation as he enquired, conversationally, 'So, this solicitor boyfriend of yours . . . is he missing you?'

Camilla spun round to look at him, blinking. 'I beg your pardon!' she exclaimed.

He was leaning casually against the wall, his fists thrust into the pockets of his jerkin, one knee slightly bent, his dark head held high as he looked down at her. 'I asked a very simple question. Is your boyfriend, Eric, missing you? I presume he must have told you when he called you at the hotel last night.'

'And what if he did?' she demanded hotly. 'What possible business might it be of yours?'

He shrugged broad shoulders. 'Just a friendly enquiry. It's nice to know someone's thinking of you when you're far away in a foreign land.'

Camilla decided to ignore the observation, and the note of mockery in his voice. Already this highly personal digression had brought a warm glow of discomfort to her skin. She said, carefully, 'I think I might be able to use this place. I'll come back for another look—alone—tomorrow morning, if that's all right?'

'Feel free.' Still, he continued to watch her, the inscrutable dark eyes relentlessly probing. Then, 'This Eric of yours . . . Is he a serious *amour*—or just a passing fancy?'

This time, she did not ignore him. Her eyes blazed her indignation at him. 'If you really want to know, he's the man I'm going to marry!' Maybe that would satisfy his perverse curiosity and put an end to his impertinent questions!

Predictably, it did not. His eyes dropped pointedly to her left hand. 'I see no engagement ring,' he pointed out. 'And I feel quite sure that this Eric of yours is the kind of man who would insist on observing such traditions.' He paused with a strangely infuriating smile. 'So why, if you're going to marry him, is there no ring?'

'Because the engagement is not yet official.'

'Ah . . .' He seemed to consider this new information. 'That must either be because he hasn't yet officially asked you, or because you have not yet officially given him your answer . . .' Boldly he held her eyes. 'Tell me, am I right?'

For some quite inexplicable reason Camilla's heart was racing, her palms grown clammy with anxiety as she balled them into tight fists at her sides. As before, when he had touched on the subject of Eric, she felt threatened and afraid. She said coldly, 'I don't intend telling you anything. It's none of your damned business!'

'Very well. Then let me guess.' His eyes wandered over her stiff, anxious form, assessing, dissecting, stripping her bare. A crude smile touched his lips as he told her, 'I say you're the one who's holding out.'

It was a coarse and inaccurate deduction, and under other more normal and benign conditions Camilla would have told him so. As it was, the one thought on her mind at that moment was, quite simply, how to escape—from the claustrophobic confines of the crypt which suddenly seemed to be closing in on her, and, above all, from the increasingly distressing proximity of this wild, outrageous man whose granite-grey eyes seemed to see right through her.

Clutching at the remnants of her disintegrating poise, she told him in a taut, hard voice, 'If you don't mind, I'd like to leave now. I think I've seen enough.'

'Are you sure?'

'Quite sure, thank you.' With his brash inquisition and uncouth insinuations he had succeeded in genuinely unsettling her, a feat that very few people these days ever managed to achieve.

He shrugged his broad frame away from the wall. 'OK. In that case, let's go.' And, just for a moment, as he straightened and nodded, Camilla dared to relax inside. Perhaps he had had enough of his game. But then, pulling the rug right out from under her, he regarded her sideways and observed, 'I'm right, aren't I? You're the one who's holding out?'

'No, I'm not, as a matter of fact!' The words shot like gunfire from her lips. 'I happen to be dead set on marrying Eric and I shall tell him so, just as soon as I return to London.'

'Why didn't you tell him before you left—if you're so dead set, as you put it?'

'Because,' she answered evenly, wondering why she was even bothering to reply, 'he gave me a week to think over his proposal. He realised it's a serious step.'

'I couldn't agree more.' But he was smiling—that mocking, superior smile of his. 'I'm sure that marriage to a man like Eric would be a very serious step indeed.'

'And what would *you* know about it? You haven't even met the man!'

'Very true,' he acknowledged. Then he paused and fixed her with that rapier-like gaze. 'I haven't met Eric, but I *have* met you.'

And what the devil was that supposed to mean? Camilla glared at him with hostile eyes, fighting against the growing unease that was prickling like cold fingers down her spine. Again that dull sense of claustrophobia was starting to close in on her.

She tore her eyes from his face. 'I've had quite enough of this ridiculous conversation! I'm getting out of here!' Giving instant substance to her words, she swung past him on perilously shaky legs and headed swiftly for the stairs.

Next minute, she was plunging into the semi-darkness, heart pumping like a steam piston inside her chest. Her hands groped for the cool, rough walls to guide her as her feet flew recklessly up the steps. Too recklessly, alas. As the stairs curved sharply, she misjudged her footing and felt her legs fold beneath her, like a deckchair.

With a strangled gasp, she staggered forwards and might have done no more than skin her knees. But at the last minute she grabbed for her camera, fearing that it might smash against the stone steps—and succeeded only in compounding the mischief, as her foot slipped yet again, sending her hurtling backwards, completely out of control. Blindly, she reached out for something to break her fall. But there was nothing there.

'Are you trying to kill yourself?'

Even as raw panic seized her, a firm hand had caught her round her middle, wrenching her upright, out of danger, and setting her down on her still-boneless feet.

'Quite an exit.' Ross sounded amused. 'Pity you had to go and spoil it rather, right there at the end.'

Camilla breathed deeply and struggled for composure, in an odd way finding his cool, detached humour more agreeable than the expected display of concern. 'Thank you,' she offered wanly, regarding with a tremor the steep descent that had almost claimed her as her eyes at last adjusted to the half-light. 'I really thought I was a goner there.'

'Then that makes two of us. Just for a moment, I was thinking that old Eric was about to be short of one bride.'

At the mention of Eric's name and the subtle note of irony in Ross's voice, Camilla's eyes darted to meet the dark gaze—alarmingly now on a level with her own as he stood on the staircase, one step below her. And she was suddenly quite overwhelmingly conscious of the easy, familiar way his arm was still wrapped around her waist. Merely to support her, she reassured herself—though the dangerous dark flicker deep in his eyes warned her she might be fooling herself.

'We couldn't have that, now, could we?' he smiled.

Camilla swallowed drily and found herself wondering why she didn't just take a prudent step away from him, to safety. One little step, that was all it required. Instead, still motionless, she heard herself asking, 'What do you mean? What couldn't we have?'

'Poor old Eric waiting at the altar and his bride lying in bits in a Highland crypt.' As he said it, he smiled lop-sidedly and his free hand reached up to touch her hair.

Camilla froze instantly, her breathing suddenly ragged and shallow, her skin strangely warm, her eyes barely focusing. Suddenly, all her senses were pinpointed on the erotically caressing fingers sending electric goosebumps across her scalp.

She swallowed helplessly as the hand on her waist drew her closer, so that she could smell the rich smell of leather, mingled with his own earthy, masculine scent. And she could neither bear to hold the burning grey gaze, nor find the strength to tear her own eyes away as, with a slow and certain inevitability, he leaned forward to claim her lips with his.

She closed her eyes with a tortured shudder as excitement, like a lance, went knifing through her, galvanising all her senses, turning her blood to molten fire. As his muscular body pressed hard against her own, driving the breath from her lungs and crushing her bones, she experienced for one glorious moment a sense of release and a sense of bondage that, curiously, were one and the same. With a sigh, she slackened and surrendered as his mouth proceeded to conquer hers.

'Camilla, Camilla . . .' His tone was husky as he murmured her name, his hand sweeping round from the small of her back to cup the taut, excited swell of her breast.

But, even as the blood leapt in her loins at the tantalising, slow caress, something akin to stunned, shocked sanity was seeping into her numbed, beleaguered brain.

With a dart of conscience she pulled away. The voice that had just murmured 'Camilla' and the lips and hands that were devouring her senses belonged to a man she scarcely knew. A man who had no right to take such liberties . . . for there was only one man in the world who did.

Dry-mouthed, trembling, hot and guilty, she wrenched herself free from his burning embrace. 'Stop!' she demanded in a rough, shaky voice. Then, like a panic-stricken beast, she turned and fled headlong away from him, up the flight of rough stone steps. And she didn't dare stop running until she was safely out of the church.

But even in the harsh light of day her heart was still hammering inside her chest, every one of her burning senses electrified and turned inside out. Never in her life before had she responded so startlingly to any man's kiss.

With an uneasy stab of conscience she admonished herself. That must be wrong. Not even to Eric's?

And all at once, a sense of dread crept like a chill wind through her bones. Not even to Eric's, an inner voice answered.

And suddenly she knew, and feared, the terrible nature of the danger she was in.

CHAPTER FOUR

NOT a single word was exchanged on the walk back from the old ruined chapel to the castle.

Stiff-legged, Camilla strode out ahead, covering the rough ground swiftly, without a thought to the damage to her shoes. And although she never once dared to glance round at Ross she could hear him following close behind on easy, long, unhurried strides that effortlessly kept pace with her own. And, as vividly as red-hot skewers, she could feel the taunting iron-grey eyes burning through the back of her neck and imagine the look of bold amusement that undoubtedly adorned his face.

That outrageous kiss and her own frantic reaction were probably his idea of a joke. She cursed him roundly beneath her breath. She must never let him catch her out like that again.

Once out in the open, away from the trees, she could feel her heartbeat begin to slow at last, and the fists that were jammed into the pockets of her trousers gradually unclenched themselves. As they came round to the front of the castle, still in single file, the hectic colour in her cheeks had subsided and she felt once more calm and in charge of herself. Half-way across the forecourt to the main door, she paused and turned to meet his eyes.

'If it's convenient, I'd like to spend some time examining the collection now. Preferably by myself,' she added pointedly, keeping her tone flat, deliberately unemotional. 'I trust you don't have any objections?'

'None at all,' he confirmed with just the hint of a smile as he stood before her, looking down, his hands in the pockets of his black leather jerkin, the wild, dark hair framing his face.

'However, I hope you won't mind if I accompany you upstairs. The key, you see. I'm afraid I can't let you have it. And if you insist on being left alone with the collection I'll also have to lock you in the room.' He raised one dark eyebrow in a mock apology. 'The insurance company, you see, would insist. I'm afraid their terms are very strict.'

Camilla kept her expression impassive. 'That's perfectly all right. I quite understand.' Though she could tell from the impish flicker in his eyes that he quite enjoyed the thought of making her his prisoner. A thought which irritated her intensely and sent an unexpected shiver of uneasiness through her. With forced lightness she put to him, 'As long as you let me out again, of course.'

'Of course.' He held her eyes for a moment and smiled. 'What possible use would you be to me locked up in a room with all the Celtic treasure? None at all,' he answered for her. 'Don't worry. I shall let you out.'

Somehow, his assurance failed to appease her. As she followed him indoors, across the hallway and up the stairs—after a brief detour to collect her camera-bag from her car—she felt sorely tempted to point out that to be of 'use' to him, as he'd so blithely put it, was the very least of her ambitions. But, of course, he was already well aware of that. He had only said it to annoy her.

At the top of the stairs he unlocked the door and stood aside to let her enter the room. 'When would you like me to come back and let you out again?' he asked.

'In a couple of hours.' She glanced at her watch. 'Half-past one or thereabouts.'

He nodded. 'Half-past one it is.' His hand was on the door-handle. 'I'll leave you now. Be good till I get back.' Then, with a wink, he closed the door. A moment later she heard the key grate in the lock, then a click of footsteps and he was gone.

She relaxed then, and looked round the room at the cabinets crammed with their Celtic treasure. For two whole hours she would be blissfully free to examine the collection and make notes and sketches and take a couple of preliminary Polaroids. She bend to unzip her camera-bag, and took out her notepad and pencil. For two whole hours there would be no Ross McKeown to ruffle her and get in her hair. Bliss. She sighed with relief. For a brief spell, at least, she could put him out of her mind.

For the next two happy hours Camilla was totally absorbed, reliving in her artist's imagination the history of the beautiful objects with which she was surrounded, all her thoughts and senses focused on the task of how to capture them on film.

She sighed as she examined a silver torque bracelet and frowned with admiration at an old Highland dirk. It was at times like these, when she had the honour of working with artefacts of such craftsmanship and beauty, that she felt truly privileged to be in the profession she was in.

She was lucky, she reminded herself. From nothing, she had built up her life exactly as she wanted it—in all areas, both professional and personal—and she must allow nothing to deflect her from her chosen path. *Nothing*, she emphasised inwardly, aware that, quite unconsciously, an image of Ross McKeown had flitted across her brain, like an interloper, shattering her inner harmony. Impatiently she chased the image away and forced her attention back to the task in hand. *Nothing*, she reminded herself ferociously. Especially not Ross McKeown!

It was a highly productive couple of hours. By the end of it Camilla had made copious notes and produced a pile of sketches of the compositions she planned to use. And she could feel her enthusiasm growing, minute by minute, for the job ahead. This commission, she was fast concluding, could prove to be not just an exciting challenge, but the jewel in the crown of her whole career.

She glanced at her watch. It was one-twenty-five, five minutes before Ross was due to come back with his precious key and let her out of here. As she bent over her camera-bag, carefully packing away her things, she was aware of a sudden stab of hunger. Little wonder, she thought to herself. Thanks to her oversleeping this morning and having to rush off without any breakfast, she hadn't eaten a bite since dinner last night. Suddenly the thought of a home-cooked lunch back at the Stag Hotel was quite enormously appealing.

She smiled in quiet anticipation. They served lunch until two-thirty. She would make it in plenty of time.

Four and a half minutes later she was waiting anxiously by the door, her ears straining for the sound of approaching footsteps. But all she could hear was the resounding silence that seemed to reverberate from the thick castle walls. And all at once she was acutely conscious of her utterly helpless, prisoner-like state.

She had tried to make light of it earlier, never believing she had anything to fear, but now she could feel a stifling anxiety beginning to creep over her and a growing sense of claustrophobia gnawing at her nerve-ends. In a rash demonstration of quite unwarranted trust, she had placed herself in Ross McKeown's hands. She might have known he could not be relied on, that he would cynically allow his promise to slip his mind—and she was stuck here, like a hamster in a cage, till he saw fit to turn up with the key.

With mounting impatience, she began to pace the floor, all her good humour melting away. What was it about the man that seemed destined to send her into a state of helpless turmoil? Just when she was starting to feel good about things, he had to go and turn them upside-down!

'It's one-thirty, Miss Holden. Are you ready to go?'

Soundlessly, without her noticing, the door had opened and he was standing there, a tall, composed figure in a burgundy-coloured shirt and jeans. With a start, Camilla swung round to face him. 'Oh, it's you!' she declared, taken unawares.

'You sound surprised. Weren't you expecting me?' He raised one sooty dark eyebrow as he spoke. 'We did say one-thirty, I believe?'

'Yes, yes, we did.' To hide her confusion, she glanced down at her watch, observing that the time was now precisely one-thirty. It would appear that, after all, he was not quite as unreliable as she had supposed. Her panic had perhaps been a trifle premature.

'So, are you ready to go? I can leave and come back later if you'd like to go on working for a while.'

'No, no. I've finished all I want to do for now.' She crossed the floor to gather up her camera-bag, slinging it across her shoulder with studied casualness. For no good reason she felt faintly foolish, as though believing he could see right through her with those penetrating iron-grey eyes and knew all about her momentary lapse of composure. Her *latest* momentary lapse, she should say. He had already witnessed quite a few.

He was standing just inside the room, leaning casually against the door-frame, the burgundy cotton of his shirt stretched tautly over the powerful lines of his shoulders as he folded his arms across his chest. He enquired with a provocative smile, 'So you're satisfied, for the moment at least?'

'Quite satisfied,' she replied, fiddling self-consciously with the strap of her camera-bag, acutely aware of the power of his presence, not quite able to meet his eyes.

'You found your solitude conducive to concentration? That's good. I too find that solitude focuses the mind.'

Camilla did not reply. Whether it was her loss of solitude that was responsible or the particular company she found herself in, she was suddenly finding it quite impossible to focus her mind on anything.

Defensively, her eyes strayed from his face—from the wide, square jaw, to the column of his throat, to the broad expanse of burgundy-clad chest.

The skin of his chest was dark from the sun and sprinkled with fine black hairs—as she could tell from the triangle of exposed tanned flesh just visible at the unbuttoned neck of his shirt. And his wrists and forearms below the turned-back sleeves were equally bronzed and sinuous and strong. With his broad shoulders, long legs and narrow hips, he had perhaps the finest physique of any man she had ever seen.

Almost idly the thought crossed her mind; then, with a sense of dazed horror, she pushed it away. Appalled at herself, she snatched her gaze upwards and, with an effort, fixed it on his face.

'I'm ready to go now,' she told him levelly. Then she took a step forward towards the door.

Ross remained exactly where he was, not exactly blocking her exit, though making it awkward for her to squeeze past. As she hesitated, he glanced round the room. 'I take it you've returned everything to its proper place.' With a lazy smile, the dark eyes raked her face and there was taunting humour in his tone as he put to her, 'I take it you're not trying to smuggle anything out in that camera-bag of yours?'

Camilla was ninety-nine per cent certain that it was intended as a joke. But it was to that one per cent of doubt that she instantaneously responded. With a deliberate gesture she swung the bag from her shoulder and almost threw it to the floor at his feet. 'Feel free to search it if you like!' she challenged. 'In fact, I absolutely insist!'

If she had responded with a simple, honest denial the matter would no doubt have ended there. But

Ross was not a man to pass up a challenge, particularly one issued with such vehemence. Keeping his eyes fixed on her face and his own features expressionless, as though carved from stone, he lowered himself down on to his haunches and pulled back the zipper of the camera-bag. 'Only too happy to oblige,' he confirmed.

Camilla watched the strong brown hands as they searched among her precious equipment, not certain with whom she felt more annoyed—herself or him. Why could nothing ever be civilised and straightforward when she was dealing with Ross McKeown? Why couldn't she simply treat him with the indifference he deserved instead of rising like a gauche fool to his every taunt?

Her eyes grazed the tightly stretched fabric of his jeans that seemed to strain against the muscular bulge of his thighs—then instantly darted away again. What was it about him that so put her on edge?

He glanced up at her, the unruly dark hair falling back from his face, the penetrating eyes beneath their straight black brows giving nothing away as he told her, 'Well, there doesn't seem to be anything here.'

Camilla glared at him. 'Did you expect there would be?'

'One never knows.' Without dropping his eyes, he pulled the zipper shut, then slowly began to rise to his feet, his tall frame seeming to unfold forever as he straightened to his full height and stood before her. 'I would say you have an honest enough face, but when dealing with strangers one can never be sure.'

That reference to her 'honest enough face' was the ultimate double-edged compliment. In essence, more of an insult, really. Camilla's brow puckered with annoyance. She straightened her shoulders and suggested caustically, 'Since you're so damned suspicious, perhaps you'd like to frisk me before you let me leave? After all, I might just have the *Ceò do dh'òr* hidden up my jumper!'

Even before the smile crossed his face—the slow and openly appreciative smile of a big cat sizing up its prey—she knew she should not have said it. She felt herself stiffen as the dark eyes swept over her, caressing the full, soft swell of her breasts beneath the bottle-green cashmere sweater, then curving past her tiny waist to the shapely hips in their jodhpur-style trousers. As his smile broadened, she prepared to take a step back. 'Is that an invitation, Miss Holden?' he enquired.

Her jaw clenched. She threw him a look of contempt. 'It most certainly is not!' she retorted.

One coal-black eyebrow lifted a fraction. He seemed to take a step towards her. 'It sounded distinctly like one to me.'

She glared at him. Don't you dare! her eyes warned. If he as much as laid one hand on her she would scream the whole damned castle down!

But already he was turning away. He threw her an amused look as he held open the door, casting one final, shamelessly appraising glance at her slender form as he observed, 'Don't worry, I won't need to frisk you, Miss Holden. I can see all too clearly what you're hiding under that sweater of yours—and it most certainly isn't the *Ceò do dh'òr*.' His gaze lingered a burning moment longer, then he motioned to her to pass ahead of him out on to the landing. 'But thanks for the offer, anyway. I may take you up on it some other time.'

Camilla's cheeks were burning as she grabbed her camera-bag from the floor, slung it hastily over her shoulder and hurried past him, eyes averted. The man's damned impertinence knew no limits! He appeared to possess not a milligram of shame!

She hovered at the top of the stairs as he pulled the door shut and locked it, watching as he slipped the key once more into the pocket of his jeans. Then, straight-backed, she preceded him down the stairs in angry silence until they reached the hall.

'So what are your plans? Will you be coming back later? I take it you're off now to have some lunch?'

As he followed her across the huge hall, she paused and turned to answer him. 'I won't be coming back today. I'd like to let my ideas settle.' Then she hurried on before he could mock her, 'If it's convenient, I'd like to start shooting early tomorrow, the earlier the better.'

With a half-smile he looked down at her and stuffed his hands into the pockets of his jeans. 'And what do you mean by early, Miss Holden. Nine o'clock, like today?'

She grimaced inwardly. 'A little earlier. I was thinking more in terms of eight.' Tonight she would be very careful to book an alarm call before she went to bed.

'Eight is fine.' As she turned away again, he followed her to the door. 'So you'll be taking the rest of the day off?' he enquired.

'From the collection, yes. But not from work.' If it was any of his damned business! She paused by the door and turned to look at him. 'I thought I might have a drive around and take some scenic pictures for my portfolio.'

'An excellent idea.' He opened up the door for her. 'There's some very pretty scenery around here. However...' he looked up at the sky and frowned a little ...'I would advise you not to venture too far. The weather can change rather abruptly in these parts and I reckon we're in for a nasty spell.' He lowered his gaze to her face once more, mocking amusement in his eyes. 'I'm sure you wouldn't want to get stranded in one of our sudden Highland mists?'

Camilla sniffed dismissively. He was simply trying to scupper her plans. Above them there was scarcely a cloud in the sky. It was a perfect autumn day. But she wasn't about to get into an argument. She threw him a bland and tolerant smile. 'Thank you for the advice. I'll see you tomorrow morning at eight.'

Then, shaking her blonde hair over her shoulders, she turned and headed for her car, her step light and a smile on her lips at the liberating prospect of an entire afternoon without the threat of Ross McKeown crossing her path.

Little did she realise that, just a matter of hours from now, she would be humming a very different tune.

On a sudden impulsive whim, Camilla decided not to take lunch at the hotel, after all. Instead, fired with sudden enthusiasm to get on with the afternoon ahead, she ordered a picnic lunch from the manageress, Mrs Cameron, then hurried upstairs to her room to change while the good woman was preparing it.

What she would do, she had decided, was drive up to Loch Maree, the spot the Laird's old gardener had particularly recommended, and have a leisurely lunch on its picturesque banks before scouting around the area for the best spots to take some scenic pictures. It would be a pleasantly leisurely afternoon. Precisely suited to her mood.

It was getting on for three o'clock by the time she came in sight of the loch and the hunger pangs were gnawing like rats at her stomach. On the road map the loch had looked much closer, a matter of twenty-odd miles away, but the bewilderingly twisting and turning road had slowed her down considerably.

Never mind, she told herself cheerfully, as she spread out the colourful tartan rug that Mrs Cameron had insisted she borrow. She was in no hurry, after all, and now she would enjoy her lunch even more!

She leaned back, tucking the skirt of the blue dress she had changed into decorously around her knees as she chewed on a chicken leg and admired the view. The old gardener hadn't been exaggerating one bit. This place just had to be one of the most beautiful spots in the world.

Happily, she drank in the view, suddenly wishing a little wistfully that Eric were there to enjoy it with her. He didn't usually care much for the great outdoors, being essentially an urban man, but she felt certain that even he would see that there was something special about this place. Then she smiled, remembering the little gift shop that she'd spied along the road. I'll stop off on my way back and buy a postcard to send him, she resolved.

She sighed happily and helped herself to another chicken leg. Suddenly, Castle Crannach and all the hassles of the past two days seemed a million miles away.

'Hi, there!'

Camilla glanced up at the sound of a voice to see a skinny, dark-haired boy, about twelve or thirteen years of age, smiling at her from the edge of the loch. He carried a fishing rod over his shoulder and he had appeared from nowhere, it seemed. As she nodded in greeting, he explained himself.

'I was up beyond those trees, looking for trout, but so far I haven't caught a thing. So I thought I'd come down here to give it a try. I'm sorry, I didn't realise you were here.'

He spoke with a typical Highland lilt, soft and musical to the ear. Camilla straightened and smiled at him. 'You're not bothering me, I promise you. Please don't feel you have to go.' In fact, she was thinking as she watched him, it would be quite pleasant to have a bit of civilised company—something she hadn't exactly enjoyed in over-abundance of late.

The boy smiled his thanks at her and squatted down to prepare his line. 'You're not from these parts, are you?' he enquired. 'Are you here on holiday?'

'Not really.' Camilla rose from her travelling rug and went down to the water's edge to join him. 'I've come here to take some photographs for a book. I'm a professional photographer.'

The boy appeared interested. 'What kind of

photographs?' Then he grinned at her as he cast his line. 'Perhaps you could take a picture of me—if I manage to catch anything!'

In the event, she did. In fact, she took several. An hour later, young Kyle, as the boy was called, was declaring his intention of adopting her as his personal good-luck charm as he posed on the lochside with his second catch. 'You should come here more often,' he told her. 'They're fighting for the fly when you're around!'

Camilla laughed and rumpled his hair, 'Don't be so modest,' she proclaimed. 'It's your dazzling technique that's responsible.'

The couple of hours they spent together were the most relaxing and congenial that Camilla had passed since her arrival in the Highlands. As Kyle helped her polish off the generous remains of her picnic lunch—Mrs Cameron had evidently assumed she had the appetite of seven men!—then took her on a guided tour of the most scenic corners of Loch Maree, Camilla could feel the tension in her gradually unloosening and that spiky, defensive state of mind that Ross McKeown had wrought in her happily begin to dissolve away. Her sense of humour was restored. She was her old good-natured self again.

It was just after five o'clock when, with a quick glance at the sky, Kyle began to pack up his fishing gear. 'Time I was getting back home,' he told her. Then he glanced up at her and warned, 'I'd advise you to get back to your hotel. I reckon we're in for a bit of a cloudburst—at the very least.'

Camilla frowned up at the sky. 'Surely not?' she protested. The sun had receded behind a bank of cloud, but they were light, fluffy clouds, not threatening at all. 'It doesn't look like rain to me.'

Smilingly, Kyle shook his head and pointed in the direction of the mountains to the west. 'That's where the bad weather's going to come from. It's been building up since just after lunchtime and it's my guess it'll be with us in less than an hour. The weather can change quite suddenly up here, sometimes without any warning at all.'

Camilla followed his pointing finger, recalling Ross's earlier warning, and she could see that beyond the range of mountains the sky looked heavy and brooding and black. But he could still have been wrong, they both could, she told herself, faintly irritated by the fact that Ross had intruded into her thoughts, and somehow even more irked by the niggling possibility that he might have been right.

Fifteen minutes later, as she and Kyle parted company—Camilla armed with the boy's address, so that she could send on the photographs to him—she made the rash and fatal mistake of allowing her irrational irritation to overrule her customary caution.

Instead of heading straight back for Glen Crannach, as her young friend had advised, out of a sense of mutiny that was entirely directed at the absent Ross she stopped off at the little gift shop on the lochside to buy a postcard for Eric, then lingered a further quarter of an hour admiring the array of pretty tartan knick-knacks that were for sale.

But the time she emerged into the street again, the sky overhead had darkened considerably and a penetrating drizzle had begun to fall. Camilla shivered as she climbed in the car. The temperature, too, had dropped abruptly. Beneath the lightweight dress she wore she could feel the goosebumps creeping over her flesh.

Still, not to worry, she consoled herself, tossing back her silky blonde hair and turning the ignition key. In just over half an hour she would be back, safe and warm, at the Stag Hotel, enjoying one of Mrs Cameron's afternoon teas.

Alas, that was not how things turned out.

Half an hour later, not only was she not back at the hotel, but she had totally lost track of where she was at all. Just a couple of miles beyond Loch Maree, the sky had suddenly turned to night and the drizzle had seemed to solidify before her eyes into a thick, impenetrable wall of fog.

She leaned forward, peering anxiously through the windscreen, as visibility dropped to a couple of yards, aware of a growing sense of panic as the fog closed around her, cutting her off. It had been difficult enough finding her way around these remote, uninhabited Highland areas in broad daylight, when she could see where she was going. In these treacherous, nightmare conditions it was an outright impossibility!

And the fog was growing thicker by the minute. She could scarcely see a foot beyond the bonnet of the car. As she came to a sudden intersection she blindly took a left, gambling on her sense of direction. If she kept calm and kept her wits about her, somehow, surely, she'd get back in one piece?

A further miserable hour later, she was finding it increasingly difficult to maintain the calmness she had vowed. She felt as though she was going round in circles and the fog was so dense she could scarcely see at all. She shivered, the tension in her mounting, as she began to fear being stranded for the night. I could die of exposure, she thought in horror, as the cold, damp air chilled her flesh. I could end up lost and alone in this wilderness and not a soul in the world would know where I was.

She breathed in deeply to stave off her panic. 'Get a grip on yourself!' she commanded.

But then, like an accursed bolt from the blue, it happened. From out of the thickening, swirling mists a dark and totally indistinguishable shape suddenly reared up in front of the car, and before she could slam her foot on the brake there was a sickening thud as she drove straight into it.

Her heart seemed to stop dead in her breast. She swallowed drily. 'Oh, no,' she breathed.

By some instinct she knew instantly that what she had hit had been a living, breathing thing. Not just some lifeless object, but vulnerable flesh and blood, like herself. In the silence that suddenly surrounded her, she dropped her head for a moment against the steering-wheel, a hollow feeling churning in her stomach, fighting back a rising sense of nausea. Whatever it was, she had probably killed it. Heaven forbid that it had been a human being.

On shaky legs, she climbed from the car and staggered round to where the creature had fallen, her eyes focusing frantically through the fog, her head swimming dizzily with apprehension.

At the sight that met her eyes, she let out a cry. Part dizzy relief, part despair, part a horrible sense of regret. Then she dropped down to her knees at its side and reached out a hand towards its face.

At least her victim had not been human. There was that much to be grateful for. But as she gazed down at the still, stricken form, sprawled out on its side on the road, Camilla felt her heart contract with pain. It was one of God's most gracious and gentle creatures, a red deer, that she had struck down.

Sudden, sharp tears pricked at her eyes. To have killed such a creature. Such horrible shame. Wretchedly, she touched with her fingertips the still-warm velvet softness of its ear and let the tears roll helplessly down her face, 'I'm sorry. So very sorry,' she whispered beneath her breath.

Then, bitterly, she wiped the tears from her cheeks. What good was sorry? The poor beast was dead.

'You bloody stupid woman! What the hell do you think you're doing?'

Still crouched on her knees, Camilla swung round, instantly recognising that voice. Then a confusion of conflicting emotions rushed through her—relief, anxiety, resentment and shame—as, an instant later, from out of the mists, the tall figure of Ross McKeown appeared.

He stood over her, glancing from her stricken, tear-stained face to the inert body of the red deer on the road. Between clenched teeth he uttered a curse, then impatiently commanded her, 'Get out of the way. Let me deal with this.'

As she staggered obediently to her feet, he was crossing to the animal and bending down, one hand expertly reaching out to press down gently on its chest. He glanced up at Camilla, his face expressionless. 'The heart's still beating. He's alive.'

Right on cue, the creature stirred, one dewy dark eye flickering open to glance up dazedly at Ross. And all at once the cold chill that had settled in Camilla's heart was replaced by a warm flood or relief. Her voice broke with happiness as she breathed, 'Oh, thank God! I didn't kill him. Do you think he's going to be all right?'

Already, Ross was helping the animal to its feet, then quickly but thoroughly checking its limbs and ribcage for damage. 'You probably did no more than stun him,' he affirmed briefly, glancing across at her. 'I presume that, considering the weather conditions, you weren't going very fast?'

'I was doing less than ten miles an hour,' she answered perfectly honestly, yet feeling the colour rise to her cheeks as she remembered his previous remarks about her driving. 'He just seemed to come out of nowhere. There was no way I could miss him.'

'He was probably as lost as you.' He threw her look of censure as with infinite gentleness and patience he guided the rapidly recovering deer to the edge of the road, then let him go. The deer shook itself, then paused to glance briefly over its shoulder before trotting off, apparently none the worse for its ordeal, away from the road and into the mists.

Ross watched the animal disappear. 'He'll go back to his herd now. He'll be OK.' And there was a note of such compassion in his voice that Camilla found herself glancing at him curiously, aware that she had just glimpsed a side of him that she had never even guessed at before.

Less than an instant later, however, the Ross McKeown who turned to face her was the one with whom she was already all too painfully familiar.

A sudden scowl darkened his features. 'So,' he said, his voice grown hard. 'Perhaps now that someone has conveniently come along to clear up your mess for you, you wouldn't mind explaining what the hell you're playing at!' As she blinked at him, momentarily taken aback, he grabbed her roughly by the arm and proceeded to lead her round the back of the car to where the Land Rover was parked. 'I thought I told you to stay close to Glen Crannach. I warned you the weather was set for a change.'

How dared he? Angrily, she snatched her arm away. 'Who do you think you are? My keeper? I don't need permission from you to go anywhere! I go where I like, when I like, thank you very much!'

'Sure you do!' His tone was shaved steel as he glared at her and grabbed her by the arm again. 'But you're not so clever at finding your way back, are you, Miss Independent!' He pulled open the Land Rover door and started to shove her unceremoniously inside. 'If I hadn't come along you would have been stuck here until the mist cleared, and sometimes these mists can last for days.'

Camilla shivered inwardly at the thought. That would have been even more unpleasant than the indignity of being saved by Ross McKeown. But only marginally, she decided, as she fought to free herself from his grip. 'What do you think you're doing?' she demanded, fighting to resist his efforts to shove her inside the car.

'What the hell do you think I'm doing? I'm taking you out of here.'

'I can go in my own car. I can follow you.'

He let out his breath in an impatient rasp. 'I'll

bet!' His tone was caustic. ' If you think I intend spending the rest of the evening playing hide and seek in the mist with you, I'm afraid you're very much mistaken. Maybe this is the sort of thing that Eric's used to, but I've had more than enough for one night!'

With one final, effortless twist of his arm, he deposited her on the passenger seat. 'Now, just do as you're told and stop arguing,' he grated. Then, before she could protest, he was stripping off his black leather jerkin, the same one he had been wearing earlier that morning, and flinging it at her as he slammed the door shut. 'And put that on,' he commanded sharply, 'before you freeze to death.'

Angrily, gratefully, Camilla did as she was told. Beneath the heat of her anger she felt shivery and cold. The jerkin was heavy and deliciously warm, with the rich, tangy scent of expensive leather mingled with Ross's own personal scent. Clean and cool and masculine. She pulled the collar up around her ears and glowered at him as he climbed in beside her a minute later, and handed her her handbag and camera-bag.

'How did you know where I was, anyway? And why did you bother to come and find me? Nobody asked you to,' she added churlishly, glowering across at him. For some reason she bitterly resented Ross McKeown in the role of knight in shining armour.

Though if a knight in shining armour was what he was, he was making no bones at all about the fact that it was a role he had stepped into reluctantly. His tone was about as chivalrous as a kick in the teeth as he informed her icily, 'When the weather changed, I phoned the hotel, just to check if you were back.' He revved the engine and glanced across at her, a black look in his eyes. 'My—gardener told me that he'd particularly recommended that you go to visit Loch Maree, so I took a gamble and headed this way. Though I may tell you, you were hard to find. You've strayed miles off the road to Glen Crannach.'

Camilla sank deeper inside the jerkin as the big car began to move away, its powerful fog-lamps piercing the gloom, as Ross stepped cautiously but confidently on the accelerator. She should thank him, of course, she was aware of that. He had saved her from a horrible ordeal. Perhaps even from an untimely death. But she felt stubbornly reluctant to acknowledge that fact. The thanks she knew she owed him remained stillborn on her lips.

He conveniently let her off the hook of gratitude with his next remark.

'You realise, of course, that the only reason I came after you was to avoid all the unpleasant fuss your disappearance would inevitably have stirred up.' There was a caustically amused note in his voice as he added, 'And, naturally, I was thinking of poor old Eric, too. Since your demise would have robbed him of a lifetime of wedded bliss, I felt it my duty, for his sake, to try and track you down.'

'How uncommonly civil of you.' Abruptly, Camilla turned away. As always, without understanding why, she had felt a tremor of anxiety at hearing Eric's name on Ross's lips. 'I'm sure he'll be eternally grateful to you.'

The rest of the journey was passed in silence, Ross concentrating on his driving, while Camilla sat huddled in her seat, staring straight ahead out into the fog. Yet, though her eyes were focused unflinchingly on the twin yellow beams cast by the headlamps, her every sense was acutely tuned to the powerful male presence at her side.

She found his nearness disconcerting, physically, emotionally, every which way. He seemed so totally, so naturally in control—as though everything he touched was at his command—and that mastery somehow threatened to spill out and draw her into its thrall.

Protectively, she wrapped her arms about her and cursed herself for her own stupidity that had dropped her into his clutches like this. She had started off celebrating her temporary release from him, and look how things had ended up!

But at least she would not be required to put up with his company for very much longer, she quietly consoled herself, as she caught a brief, reassuring glimpse of a signpost announcing, 'Glen Crannach, five miles'. Soon she would be back at the Stag Hotel, belatedly enjoying that soothing cup of tea that she had earlier promised herself.

At least, that was what she was thinking—until he took a deliberate turning in the opposite direction to the hotel.

She snapped her head round to look at him, a flash of anxiety igniting in her breast. 'You're going the wrong way,' she informed him. 'The road to the Stag Hotel was back there.'

Iron-grey eyes swivelled round to fix her. His tone was flat. 'I'm aware of that. However, my dear Miss Independent, I'm afraid I have not the faintest intention of further putting myself about by escorting you all the way back to the hotel. We're going straight back to the castle.'

He paused and smiled a vampire's smile. 'Out of the goodness of my heart, I've decided to let you spend the night as my guest!'

CHAPTER FIVE

OUT of the goodness of his heart, my eye! Camilla was thinking sourly to herself as they came to Castle Crannach at last and the Land Rover drew up outside. The only reason he was forcing her to spend the night at the castle was because she had expressed a preference to go back to the hotel. His motivation, in other words, was nothing but typical sheer bloody-mindedness!

He had gone to the trouble of rescuing her—reluctantly, on his own admission—and now he was making her pay the price of her transgression!

He led her upstairs to a part of the castle she had never been in before, along corridors of velvet-soft, deep crimson carpet, past walls lined with paintings in heavy gilt frames, to a room at the end beyond a carved oak door. He thrust the door open and ushered her inside. 'The rose room,' he announced. 'At your disposal for the duration of your stay.'

My *brief* stay, she amended to herself. My exceedingly brief and reluctant stay. Aloud, she told him, 'How very kind.' Her tone was heavily sarcastic. As she spoke, she kept her eyes fixed on his face, not even bothering to glance round the room.

'I trust you'll find it comfortable.' A flicker of amusement touched his eyes. The situation, evidently, appealed to his mawkish sense of humour.

Camilla stared back at him in silence, her own expression fixed and stony.

He was standing casually in the doorway, hands loosely in the pockets of his jeans, the thick, soft, deep red sweater he wore pushed half way up his strong, tanned forearms. At a guess, she would say that he wore nothing under it. Between the loose round neck and the column of his throat only a few dark hairs were visible. She could imagine, without any effort at all, the broad, sun-darkened expanse of chest, hair-roughened and muscular, that lay beneath.

She dropped her gaze away, her colour rising. What the devil had got into her? She was stripping the wretched man with her eyes!

He shifted slightly to lean one shoulder against the door-frame. 'I'm going to be busy, I'm afraid, so I won't be able to have dinner with you. You can dine alone in the dining-room downstairs or I can have Maggie bring something up here.'

As he paused, waiting for an answer, Camilla raised her eyes to his. 'I think I'd prefer to eat in my room. Then I'll just go straight to bed.'

'As you wish. I'll inform the staff.'

He didn't move, just stood there looking at her, a tall, powerful figure, faintly threatening. Though the threat he posed was not so much physical, it was less easily defined, almost emotional. It was the way he was standing there, blocking her exit, somehow seeming to hem her in. She could feel that sense of control that he exuded reaching out, as if to claim her, just as she had done earlier in the Land Rover. The feeling was claustrophobic. It filled her with alarm.

She took a deep breath, composing herself, then let her eyes glide to the door. 'Perhaps you could leave me now? I'd very much like to take a shower.'

As he straightened, she relaxed a bit, assuming he was about to oblige. But then, instead of stepping out into the corridor, he took a step further into the room. She stiffened as he came to stand over her. 'Aren't you forgetting something?' he smiled.

Her flesh tingled strangely as she blinked up into his eyes, those dark, piercing eyes that seemed to see right through her. Then she swallowed drily. 'What have I forgotten?' Her mind was flying back to that incident in the chapel, as, still smiling, he reached out one hand towards her.

'This.' There was an endless moment of suspense before his fingers softly touched the lapel of the black leather jerkin she had forgotten she was wearing, and she imagined she could feel the animal warmth of them searing through the soft fabric into her flesh. For a moment he allowed his hand to linger, the dark eyes provocative as they burned into hers. 'It looks very good on you, I confess, but I'm afraid I have to ask for it back.'

'Of course!' At once, she was struggling out of the garment, felling foolish, embarrassed by her own gaucheness. She thrust it at him. 'I quite forgot. Thank you for letting me use it.'

He eyed her closely. 'Don't mention it.' Then he slung the jerkin casually over his shoulder, the glossy black of the leather reflecting against the dark gloss of his hair. Without further ado, he turned to the door. 'I'll leave you to get on with your shower. I'll tell Maggie to look out some pyjamas when she brings you up your dinner. There are bound to be some of my sister's somewhere.'

As she nodded her thanks, he stepped out into the corridor. 'I'll see you at breakfast,' he told her with a smile. 'That is, of course, if you're up in time.'

Then, a moment later, the bedroom door closed and she was left alone.

Camilla didn't take her shower immediately. Instead, she sat down on the edge of the bed and took from her bag the postcard she had bought for Eric on her way back from Loch Maree and proceeded to write a long, affectionate message on the back. For suddenly she was filled with an urgent and overwhelming need to communicate with him. Somehow to bring him closer to her. To fend off the threat that she could feel closing in.

Later, when she had eaten, as she crawled beneath the rose-coloured sheets, dressed in the pretty broderie anglaise nightdress that Maggie had brought her, she propped the postcard carefully against the bedside table lamp. Like a talisman, or a string of garlic, that might protect her from some impending doom.

Then, for a long time before she finally turned out the light, she lay against the big, soft pillows, staring fixedly at it, struggling desperately to banish the troubling dark thoughts that invaded her mind.

'Eric. Eric,' she whispered over and over, like an incantation, to the empty room.

But it was a picture of Ross McKeown, with his wild, dark hair and piercing grey eyes, that still stubbornly refused to be banished from her mind as she drifted at last into fitful sleep.

* * *

Camilla awoke next morning just after seven.

After a night spent restlessly tossing and turning, she was feeling even more exhausted than she had the night before, but it was a relief to get up and get started with the day.

She hurried through to the adjoining bathroom and showered quickly, then pulled on her clothes—the same blue dress of the day before—then briskly brushed back her glossy blonde hair and made her way downstairs.

It would only be polite, she had decided, at least to go through the motions of accepting her host's invitation to breakfast. With a bit of luck, he would not actually be there. He would already have finished ages ago.

Alas, however, he had not.

She walked into the breakfast-room, following a mouth-watering aroma of bacon and warm toast, to find him seated at the long oak breakfast-table, dressed in a dark blue roll-neck sweater and pouring coffee from a huge silver pot. But he was not alone. She stopped in her tracks, frowning as she recognised the old man seated opposite him. Even without the battered old hat he'd been wearing last time they'd met, she recognised him instantly. The heir to Castle Crannach, it appeared, was having breakfast with his gardener!

Ross glanced up at her as she hovered in the doorway. 'Good morning, Miss Holden. Come and join us.' Then, as she did so, hesitantly, seating herself as far away from him as she possibly could without appearing obvious, he went on with a wicked smile, 'I believe you two have already met, but I don't believe you've been introduced . . .'

As she turned to meet the eyes of the old gentleman, who glanced up now from his bacon and eggs, Camilla had a sudden premonition of what was coming next. She tied a tight smile to her lips and waited as Ross continued, 'Miss Holden, meet my grandfather. Grandfather—Miss Camilla Holden.'

So, her somewhat belated premonition had been absolutely right, after all! Just as she had when she'd first met Ross, mistaking him for a lowly shepherd, she'd made a totally wrong, perhaps even insulting assumption about his grandfather's identity. In her dealings with these McKeowns she seemed destined not to put a foot right!

Pink embarrassment stained her cheeks as, avoiding Ross's amused and mocking eyes, she turned apologetically towards the old man. 'I'm sorry, last time we met I had no idea you were the Laird. I thought——' Abruptly she broke off, fearing she might merely compound the damage if she attempted to explain herself.

But the old man was smiling at her without a trace of censure in his eyes. He held out one gnarled and weatherbeaten hand. 'I was having a day off from being the Laird last time we met,' he explained. He winked at her and introduced himself less formally.

'Angus McKeown,' he announced. 'I'm delighted to renew our acquaintance.'

Just as she had that last time, by the rhododendrons, Camilla found the old man full of easy warmth and good humour. Not in the least like his overbearing grandson, she reflected wryly to herself as, soon, the two of them were chatting away quite happily, as though they'd known one another for years.

Ross remained with them only long enough to finish his coffee. As the old Laird plied her with questions about her life and her work in London, she was aware, from the corner of her eye, of his grandson watching her with that habitual look of superior amusement on his face. She felt quietly relieved when he started to leave.

'I've arranged for a couple of my men to go and pick up your car this morning. You can wait for it here, if you want, or if you'd rather go straight back to the hotel I can ask them to drop it off there.'

Camilla swivelled round to look at him, realising that he was talking to her. A faintly guilty blush stained her cheeks. The truth was, she hadn't given the fate of her hire car a second thought. Somehow, quite unconsciously, she'd just assumed that Ross would deal with that—and the realisation of that assumption all at once made her feel uncomfortable. She had no right, nor any wish, to make such assumptions where he was concerned.

'Thank you,' she told him politely, then added, 'I'd prefer it if they just brought it here. I thought I might take advantage of the early start by getting some more pictures done. Some outdoor shots, I thought, if that's all right with you.'

'Very well.' He glanced at his watch. 'My grandfather has the key. He can let you into the collection. I'm afraid I have work to do.' The iron-grey eyes held hers for a moment. 'However, I must insist that you wait to do the *Ceò do dh'òr* until either myself or Maggie is available. Today, I'm afraid, is Maggie's day off and I am going to be rather busy.'

He cast an affectionate smile in the direction of
the old Laird. 'I'm sure my grandfather would be
only too willing to do the honours himself, but I'm
afraid I can't allow such an imposition. His health
of late has been a cause for some concern. It would
be too much to expect him to run around after you
as bodyguard to the jewels.'

'But of course! I wouldn't dream——' Camilla
flashed a glance of concern at the old man, then
turned back to Ross again. 'I wasn't planning to do
the *Ceò do dh'òr.* I think I'll probably leave that till
last.'

'In that case, you're free to come and go as you
please. Though, naturally,' he reminded her with
just a touch of gravel in his voice. 'I expect you to
treat even the less valuable items with due care and
respect.'

As he pushed back his chair and prepared to
leave them, Camilla met his gaze but did not reply.
She felt faintly offended by that cautionary remark.
Didn't he know he could trust her absolutely on
that score?

And perhaps that was why her tone was laced
with just a hint of defensive abrasiveness as she
asked, 'Have you any idea when my car might be
back? I'd like to nip back to the hotel at some point
and change into fresh clothes.'

'Then I'm afraid you'll just have to wait until it's
convenient for one of my men to go and pick it up.
Either that or take a taxi.' The touch of gravel in his
voice had turned to cut glass now. The dark eyes
flashed at her with impatience. 'It may come as a
nasty shock, Miss Holden, but some of us have

better things to do than run around at your convenience.'

As he turned and strode out of the room on long legs, stiff with irritation, the old Laird paused to watch him go, then turned to the suddenly flush-faced Camilla with a sympathetic smile.

'He doesn't mean to be brusque,' he assured her. 'It's just that right now he's got a lot on his plate. Running Castle Crannach estate single-handed, as he insists on doing, is no mean feat, I assure you. And he worries about me, especially since my illness.' He smiled at Camilla, urging her indulgence. 'Believe me, he's got a lot on his mind.'

For the old Laird's sake, Camilla forced a smile. 'I'm sure he has,' she agreed politely. Though privately, angrily, she was thinking that it was his grandson's innate lack of civility, not any overload of pressures from outside, that was responsible for the roughness of his tongue. In spite of his lofty social status, when it came to manners he was a semi-barbarian. That was all there was to it. Pure and simple.

The old Laird leaned back in his seat and threw her a confiding smile. 'Of course, it's in his nature as well. He always did tend to take on too much, even as a child. He never was one to turn down a challenge, no matter what the risks or sacrifice involved.'

As the old man fondly shook his head, Camilla had a sudden vivid vision of the recalcitrant Ross as a young boy. All wild hair and boundless energy, up to every mischief he could find. In spite of herself, she smiled a small smile. It was an image that, illogically, she found faintly endearing.

Angus McKeown ran one sun-browned hand across his silvery hair. 'He's always been one to live life to the hilt, always in search of a bit of excitement. Even when it comes to his so-called leisure.' He sighed a little and shook his head. 'One would hardly describe motorbike racing as a relaxing pursuit, now, would one?' he asked rhetorically.

'Motorbike racing?' Camilla frowned. 'You mean that bike he arrived on yesterday—he uses that for racing?'

'It's his great passion. And he's damned good, too. Most people are tipping him for the local championship this year.'

Camilla's eyes widened. So Ross McKeown's idea of a bit of quiet relaxation was hurtling round a dusty racetrack on two wheels at a hundred miles an hour. Somehow the picture that conjured up in her mind fitted perfectly with her image of the man. Yet she couldn't help but quietly reflect that motorbike racing hardly seemed like a sensible pastime for a man with a curse hanging over his head!

But then, that was strictly his affair, she told herself hurriedly as concern lanced through her. He had told her he didn't believe in curses, and it was hardly her place to do his worrying for him!

She glanced up now as his grandfather leaned across the table towards her. 'Will you still be around next Friday?' he wanted to know.

Camilla nodded. 'I should be, yes. I plan to go back to London that weekend.'

'Good.' The white head nodded, pleased. 'In that case, you're cordially invited to join the celebrations for my seventy-eighth birthday. We're having a little party. Just family, you understand. I'd be honoured if you'd attend.'

'And I'd be more than honoured to do so,' she answered, genuinely flattered. Though it crossed her mind that there was at least one person who would be less than delighted by her presence at the party—and, perversely, that knowledge only made her look forward to the evening even more.

After breakfast, the old Laird accompanied her to the room where the collection was kept, then waited as she gathered up the various pieces that she planned on shooting outside.

As she did so, she noticed, with some irritation, that the carved box containing the *Ceò do dh'òr* was no longer in the cabinet where it had been before. Ross had evidently returned it to the safe. So why had he bothered to make an issue of the fact that he didn't want her to shoot it today, when she didn't have access to it anyway? Easy, she answered herself. It was just another example of his difficult and contrary turn of mind!

The Laird went off to sit quietly in the conservatory for a while. 'Just give me a shout when you need me to perform my duty as keeper of the keys again,' he smiled. 'I'm more than happy to oblige.'

But Camilla didn't intend bothering him again for quite a while. 'What I've got here will keep me busy for a couple of hours. You just relax,' she advised him.

She took the pieces she had chosen down to a secluded corner of the garden, to the old sundial that she had mentally earmarked as a possible location the previous day, and began to set up her first picture of the day.

Just as she had suspected, it was an ideal spot. The rough stone of the body of the sundial, shot through with glistening earthy lights, provided a perfect complement to the elaborately worked silver of the pieces themselves, while the essential concept embodied in the old sundial seemed to make an appropriate statement about the timeless quality of their beauty.

Mysteriously, the passage of time had simply added lustre to their appeal.

She was right in her prediction that she would be fully occupied for the next couple of hours. It was just after ten o'clock when she finally wound up her last roll of film and deposited it, with a satisfied smile, in the front pocket of her camera-bag. A good job well done, she congratulated herself. Instinctively, she just knew that the pictures she had taken would turn out well.

But the morning was still young, and now that she had got into her stride she had every intention of keeping going. She would return what she had shot so far to the safety of the collection room and select some more pieces to shoot elsewhere. With any luck, her car would have been returned by now, and she had loads more film stowed away in the boot. If not, she would take a quick taxi ride into the village and stock up there.

Carefully she loaded up her camera-bag and slung it, with its broad strap, over her shoulder. Then, humming happily to herself, she set off across the grounds towards the main entrance of the castle. She'd only got about half way there when she heard the shouting.

A man's voice, full of concern. 'Somebody, quick! Get a doctor!' A car's engine revving, a scuffle of footsteps, then more shouting. 'What's happened? Is he all right?'

Quite involuntarily, Camilla's steps quickened. Entirely of their own accord her finger tightened around the strap of her bag and a sudden, swift shaft of anxiety went piercing through her breast.

And somehow she knew, by some strange intuition, as she sprinted up the stone steps from the garden, what manner of horror awaited her at the top. Though she was not prepared for the rush of emotion, like a fist being driven straight into her stomach, that went charging through her at the sight that met her eyes.

Ross. Doubled up and bleeding, being helped out of a transit van. And the dark blue sweater he had been wearing virtually torn off his back.

Just for a fraction of a second Camilla paused at the top of the steps, oddly winded by the sight. Then she was running towards him as the two men with him began to assist him towards the main door of the castle.

'What happened?' she blurted out. 'Ross, are you all right?'

As she came level with him, he had already freed himself from the assisting hands of his two companions and was determinedly making his own independent way to the front door. Typical! she thought to herself with a quick dart of impatience, then instantly felt her heart contract as he swivelled round to look at her, his face as pale as parchment beneath the darkness of his tan.

He smiled, a crooked, self-mocking smile. 'I had a bit of a fight with a tractor,' he told her. 'And if you think I look bad, you should see the tractor!'

One of the two men chipped in. 'You could have been killed, sir,' he protested. 'It's a bloody miracle that you weren't.' He turned a pair of concerned eyes on Camilla. 'The damned thing just set off across the field on its own, no one at the controls, it was the weirdest thing. If I hadn't seen it with my own eyes, I swear to you, I would never have believed it.' He shook his sandy head and frowned. 'It was as though it suddenly had a will of its own. It went heading straight for Mr McKeown.'

Ross shook his dark head. 'Some fault in the electrical system,' he offered by way of explanation. 'I hardly think it likely that it was out to settle some personal grudge.'

In spite of his light, dismissive tone and his determination to shrug off the incident, Camilla could see by the knit of his brows that he was in considerable pain. As they reached the front door, she stole a glance at his shoulder, where most of the damage appeared to have been done. It looked in need of urgent attention. 'Has someone sent for a doctor?' she demanded.

The sandy-haired man nodded. 'Dave's gone to fetch Dr Fraser. His surgery's just a couple of miles down the road. He should be here any minute.'

'Good.' As the two men began to take their leave, without even thinking what she was doing Camilla followed Ross protectively into the hall, her eyes on the torn and blood-soaked sweater that hung in shreds from his wounded shoulder. 'In the meantime, while we're waiting, I think I should have a go at cleaning you up.'

'I didn't realise that among your many talents you also possess a nursing certificate.' Ross paused in the hallway and looked down at her with a taunting expression in his iron-grey eyes. But if it was in his mind to reject her offer, he was momentarily diverted as the phone began to ring.

A minute or two later, he laid down the receiver. 'That was Mrs Fraser. Her husband's in the village delivering a baby. He won't be able to get here for at least an hour.' He smiled a lopsided smile. 'It looks, my dear Miss Holden, as though I'm obliged to accept your offer after all.'

Levelly, Camilla returned his gaze. 'Don't worry, I know what I'm doing. I don't possess a nursing certificate, but I did do a course in first aid once. I assure you, I'm fairly competent in the basics of treating a wound.'

Fifteen minutes later, through in the drawing-room and armed with a pile of big, soft towels, a bowl of warm water, antiseptic and cotton wool, she was ably demonstrating her skills. Ross had stripped off the bloodstained sweater and was straddling, back to front, one of the delicate Sheraton chairs, his arms draped loosely over its back.

Camilla stood behind him, carefully cleaning around the wound with sure but delicate strokes. And it was a mess, she observed to herself, her lips pursing with sharp concern as she surveyed the torn flesh of his shoulder and the dark bruise that spread down his muscular arm. But, anxious not to alarm her patient, she told him kindly, 'It'll be all right, but you may well need a couple of stitches.'

He shrugged indifferently. 'I'll survive,' he said.

That fact was not in question. Camilla smiled quietly to herself, feeling a sneaking sense of relief that he was bearing up so well. Already, he seemed to have totally recovered from the initial shock of the accident. It would, apparently, take a great deal more than an encounter with a three-ton tractor to put Ross McKeown out of action!

But, of course, she should have known that. Ross was a survivor. Something we have in common, she found herself musing with a quiet smile, as her fingers worked delicately against his smooth skin. And though, on the surface, it was an alien thought, it was at the same time oddly warming to discover that they might have something in common after all.

Almost worriedly, she shook the thought off. This sudden physical intimacy between them was doing strange things to her head! In fact the whole unfortunate incident had triggered off a series of emotional responses in her that were inappropriate and out of place. That rush of concern she had experienced at the sight of him, that tug at her heart on seeing he was hurt, now that she considered it, made no sense. Why should she care in the slightest about him when all he ever did was make her life difficult?

Because I'm a normal, compassionate human being, she instantly chided herself in defence. Hadn't she felt exactly the same thing for the red deer last night? And what she was doing now she would have done for anyone. There was nothing strange or out of place about it. It was no more than a simple, impersonal kindness from one human being to another.

Still, she was mildly relieved when her task was done. Taking care that her fingers came into contact with his flesh as briefly as possible, she laid a soft pad of lint across the wound, and strapped it in place, to keep it clean. 'That'll do as a temporary dressing, until the doctor comes.' Then, abruptly, she turned her attention to clearing up the first aid things.

He stood up and turned round to look at her, unstraddling his long legs from the seat of the chair. 'Thanks, Camilla. I'm most grateful,' he told her, addressing her informally for the very first time. 'If I had to have a fight with a tractor, I'm glad I did it when you were around.'

Fumblingly she rolled up the gauze, avoiding contact with his eyes, wishing she weren't quite so aware of the muscular expanse of naked chest standing less than an arm's length away. He was every bit as splendidly built as she had secretly imagined he would be.

'Don't mention it,' she mumbled, forcing her attention on to the gauze and away from his all-too-near physique. Then she added, as a thought occurred to her, 'How on earth could a tractor just come rolling across a field on its own?'

'That's something we'll have to investigate. I reckon it was a fault in the electrical system.'

Yes, that was the excuse he had given before, but Camilla had her own private theory. Obliquely, she asked him, 'Have you ever heard of such a thing happening before?'

'Not to me, personally. But I know that such things can happen.'

She half turned then to look at him. 'Don't you think it's a little odd?'

'Odd?' Ross met her eyes and smiled. 'Are you thinking what I think you're thinking? Are you suggesting it was the *Ceò do dh'òr* curse?'

A touch defensively she straightened. 'Well, it might have been.'

But he shook his head. 'Surely, if it had been the curse, I would have been dead, not just slightly wounded? These ancient Celtic curses don't fool around, you know.'

There was a gently mocking note in his voice that told her he was not taking her suspicions seriously. And he was probably right. She was merely being fanciful. On a more down-to-earth note, she observed, 'I noticed you've taken the precaution of returning the jewels to the safe.'

'The *Ceò do dh'òr*? What do you mean?' Suddenly, he was frowning at her. 'I haven't put them back in the safe. I left them in the cabinet with the other jewels.'

'Well, they weren't there this morning I can most definitely assure you of that.'

'Show me.' Without pausing for breath, he turned and strode across the room. 'Come!' he commanded as she began to follow him. 'I think we'd better check it out right now.'

She'd been absolutely right, of course. As she'd observed that morning, the box containing the *Ceò do dh'òr* was no longer in the cabinet with the other jewels. Even more peculiar, and alarming, when Ross opened up the safe it was not in there either.

'Perhaps your grandfather removed it,' she suggested as he stared, uncomprehending, at the empty space, his features darkening into a scowl.

Ross shook his head. 'He wouldn't do that without telling me. And no one else is allowed to handle them.'

She stated the obvious. 'Well somebody has.' Then she elaborated boldly as, in a sudden flash of intuition, an explanation occurred to her. 'I bet I know where they are—back on that island you told me about, the island where they were originally kept!'

He regarded her closely, still frowning. 'The Isle of Mhoire? What makes you think that?'

'Why, it's obvious!' Camilla declared, her enthusiasm growing as she went on. 'That's why your accident wasn't fatal, as the curse intended it to be. By the time the tractor hit you, the jewels were already back on the island where they're supposed to be. I'll bet you anything that's what happened. After all, you said yourself that the curse only came about because the jewels were taken away!'

Excitedly, she paused for breath, aware that what she was saying sounded like a fairy-tale, yet utterly convinced that she was right.

For a moment, Ross said nothing. He slammed shut the door of the empty safe. 'That's as maybe,' he remarked, seeming to dismiss her theory out of hand. 'But before we start getting bogged down in legend, I think we'd better call the police.'

The next few hours were chaos.

First, Dr Fraser appeared, to praise Camilla's first aid efforts and put a couple of stitches in Ross's wound. Then the police arrived and asked endless questions, to which, apparently there were no answers. Old Angus knew nothing of the fate of the

Ceò do dh'òr and Maggie, the housekeeper, the only other person who had access to a strong-room key, was having a day off and could not be traced. When the police finally left, Camilla left, too. She was no longer in the mood for taking pictures and there seemed little point in hanging around.

She was back at the Stag Hotel, getting ready for dinner that evening when the phone on the bedside table rang. She picked up the receiver, assuming it would be Eric, and was surprised when Mrs Cameron in reception informed her, 'There's a visitor for you, Miss Holden. Mr Ross McKeown. I've sent him up.'

Camilla frowned as she laid down the phone. What the devil was going on? And what did Ross mean by turning up here at the hotel like this?

She did not have long to wait for her answer. A sharp tap sounded on the door. Then, even before she had pulled it half open, he was striding purposefully into the room.

She rounded on him. 'What the devil——?' But that was as far as she got.

Like some wild warrior, he turned to face her, hands on hips, his dark head thrown back. 'Pack a case,' he commanded, 'and prepare yourself for a spot of adventure. First thing tomorrow morning you and I are sailing to the Isle of Mhoire!'

CHAPTER SIX

THERE had been absolutely no point in trying to argue with him. Ross had suddenly decided, so he had explained, that Camilla's intuition was worth following up. And in his usual impetuous way, no sooner had he decided than he was ready to act.

His insistence that she accompany him he had justified thus: 'If the jewels *are* on the island—which you seemed so sure about this afternoon—you'll have a unique opportunity to photograph them in their original setting. Surely a professional like yourself couldn't throw up an opportunity like that?'

He was right, she couldn't. And besides, in itself, the prospect of a trip to the romantic Isle of Mhoire really rather excited her. What filled her with considerably less enthusiasm was the identity of her travelling companion. He had warned her they would be away for at least two days. The prospect sent shivers down her spine.

Nevertheless, packed and ready, just after nine o'clock next morning, Camilla called Eric's office in London to advise him of this unexpected development, only to be told by his secretary that he was in an early-morning meeting.

As she left a message with the girl, she kicked herself mentally. She should have called him at home last night, or earlier this morning, as soon as she got up. What on earth was he going to think when his secretary passed on the message that his fiancée-to-be had suddenly decided to go off to the Hebrides with the disreputable grandson of the Laird of Glen Crannach?

As she waited now in her hotel-room for Ross to come and pick her up, she checked her reflection in the mirror. She had opted for a workmanlike pair of cord trousers, in a plain grey colour, the same as her sweater, and she had drawn back her shiny blonde hair, almost severely, in a clasp at her nape.

She had also elected to wear no make-up, no jewellery, and plain flat pumps. This was a business excursion, pure and simple. Let Ross McKeown be in no doubt about that.

He arrived outside the Stag Hotel at nine-thirty on the dot, precisely as they had arranged, and deposited her bag in the back of the Land Rover, alongside his own.

'How's your shoulder?' she enquired politely, as he climbed in beside her and they set off. 'Did you manage to sleep last night?'

He smiled across at her. 'Like a log. It feels a little stiff today, but I can't complain.'

He certainly didn't look as though it was causing him any discomfort. Dressed in a heavy deep red sweater that enhanced and dramatised his dark good looks, and a pair of his customary jeans, he looked the picture of health and fitness. He probably always did, she mused, quite unable to envisage him in the passive role of invalid. A strong constitution and an iron will would ensure he never had to play that unlikely part for long!

They were heading westwards towards the coast. 'We'll drive down to Gairloch,' he informed her, 'and pick up the ferry there. There's one goes to the

Isle of Mhoire about lunchtime, I believe. Though it doesn't go direct. We'll have to stop off at about half a dozen other little islands on the way. With any luck, we should get there by teatime.'

'Teatime!' Camilla threw him an impatient look. She had anticipated that their voyage would take less than an hour. 'Wouldn't it be simpler to take a ferry that goes to the island direct, rather than all that messing about?'

He nodded. 'You're right, it would.' Then he turned to fix her with iron-grey eyes, a devilish smile curling round his lips. 'The trouble is, there is no direct ferry. In fact, we're lucky to be able to catch today's. The ferry service to the Isle of Mhoire only runs a couple of days a week.'

'You're joking!' She blinked at him, knowing he was not. Suddenly, she understood why he had warned her they would be away for a couple of days at least.

He shook his head. 'This isn't the London commuter service, with ferries every half-hour. The islanders lead an isolated life, and that's the way they seem to want it. No telephones, no TV, a mail service only once a week. It was only just over five years ago that they elected to have electricity installed.'

Camilla blinked at him again. What sort of primitive, backward place was he taking her to? she wondered. 'But this is the last quarter of the twentieth century! Surely people don't still live like that?'

'There they do. But they live well. You'll be surprised when you see for yourself.'

Suddenly, in spite of herself, Camilla was doubly

curious. She had never visited such a place before, and, as Ross had warned her last night, it promised to be something of an adventure. Yet in spite of her excitement she felt a growing unease.

In such a place, someone such as herself, used to every modern convenience, would be forced to rely utterly on someone like him, who knew his way around, who knew how things worked. She would be totally dependent on him, and that prospect appealed to her not one bit.

But, short of demanding that he let her out of the car and carry on without her, there wasn't a great deal she could do. Not if she wanted to shoot the *Ceò do dh'òr*, for she was still quite certain that it was on the island.

Resignedly, she sat back in her seat as they headed for Gairloch and the point of no return. Let's just hope this doesn't turn out to be *too* much of an adventure! she was thinking to herself.

The little ferry with its cargo of just three vehicles and a score of passengers set sail shortly after twelve o'clock.

Camilla leaned against the guard rail to watch the noisy convoy of seagulls that escorted the little ferry as it chugged out of the tiny harbour. Then she sighed and let her gaze drift back to the rapidly receding coastline with its clutter of little grey stone buildings twinkling in the low autumn sun and, behind them, brooding and protective, the cloud-capped peaks of the Western Highlands.

She closed her eyes and lifted her face up to the wind, a kindly, gentle westerly breeze that caught at the loose strands of her hair and made them dance like gold threads in the sun.

Unaccountably, she felt good. This place that, just a couple of days ago, had seemed so alien, so strange, had somehow, much to her surprise, wormed its way into her heart. As the clean salt tang of the sea filled her lungs, she breathed in deeply and smiled. It was all so different from what she was used to, but at this moment she would not have been anywhere else.

With a stab of guilt, she thought of Eric, stuck in the pulsing mèlée of London, his ears assaulted by the roar of the traffic, his nostrils by the stench of fumes, as he battled his way to some crowded restaurant for a hurried lunch. Then she smiled to herself. The truth was, Eric thrived on that, just as she had always done. He would be amused if he could see her now. This sudden taste for the rural life was a side of her he had never seen.

But this peaceful interlude could not last.

'So what does boyfriend Eric think of you coming away with me?' Just as she had almost managed to blot his existence out of her mind, Ross was standing right beside her, by some fluke appearing to read her mind.

She turned her head briefly to glare at him. Earlier he had been chatting to the ferryman, and she had been hoping he might stay thus occupied for the remainder of the voyage. She pushed the loose strands of hair from her face. 'I don't know what you mean,' she said.

He leaned casually against the guard rail, the dark hair whipping in the wind, and regarded her with a look of amusement. 'I take it you did let Eric know that you were coming away with me?'

'Of course.' She narrowed her eyes at him, not quite certain if she cared for his choice of phrase, at the same time feeling that familiar tension that instantly knotted inside her whenever he mentioned Eric's name. Something which he did with such casual familiarity that she felt faintly thrown as to how to respond. He referred to Eric as though he knew him personally and, uncomfortably, that seemed to close the distance between them. In a conscious effort to widen the gap, she turned her attention back to the sea.

'Are you hungry?'

'A little.' In all the excitement, she had quite forgotten about her stomach, but by now it was at least five hours since she had eaten breakfast. Just the mere suggestion of the subject of food had awakened a ravenous, gnawing pang.

'Let's eat, then.' Ross held up the plastic bag he was carrying in one hand. While they were waiting to load the car on to the ferry, he had disappeared off into the village and reappeared fifteen minutes later, carrying this unidentified package. He hadn't said what it contained and Camilla hadn't asked. She was relieved now to discover that, in whatever basic form, it appeared to contain their lunch.

He led her to a quiet corner of the deck and sat down on one of the slatted wooden benches. Then, as she sat down beside him, but not too close, he proceeded to amaze her by laying on the bench before her a mouth-watering selection of crispy filled rolls, a lump of cheese and some shiny red apples, plus a thermos flask of coffee. He grinned at her with the self-satisfied air of a magician producing rabbits from out of a hat. 'Hey presto!

Help yourself,' he invited, watching her.

She selected one of the rolls, crammed with thick slices of honey-roast ham, tomatoes and a generous dollop of home-made chutney, and sank her teeth into it gratefully. It was melt-in-the-mouth delicious.

'OK?' he wanted to know, as he poured coffee for both of them and helped himself to one of the rolls.

She nodded enthusiastically. 'Excellent,' she confirmed between chews.

'Not quite the sort of lunches I'm sure you're used to enjoying with Eric, but it won't do you any harm to rough it just for once.'

The sarcastic humour in his voice made her glance round at him. She could see the same sarcastic humour reflected in his eyes. One dark eyebrow was lifted speculatively as he watched her. He was mocking her as usual. Camilla felt her anger rise.

She laid down her roll and looked straight back at him. 'You're wrong about me, you know,' she told him.'

'Wrong?' He took a mouthful of his roll. 'Tell me, in what respect?'

'In just about every respect I can think of.' She hesitated, wondering if she should continue. Her background was something she rarely spoke of and it was really none of Ross McKeown's business. But something urged her to go on. 'You seem to think of me as some kind of spoiled and pampered brat. Someone who's had things easy all her life. Well, nothing could be further from the truth.'

Attentively, the grey eyes watched he. He neither confirmed nor denied her accusation.

Stiffly, Camilla continued, 'My mother died when

I was seven. I never even knew my father. I was brought up in a series of children's homes and foster homes in one of the poorer parts of London—a million light years away from Knightsbridge, where you seem to think I belong. Believe me, when it comes to roughing it, there's absolutely nothing you can teach me.'

As she came to the end of her brief resumé, her fists were clenched and her heart was beating hard, as it always did when she remembered these things. To hide her emotion she dropped her eyes to her lap and waited in a silence that seemed to go on forever.

Then, at last, Ross spoke. 'I'm sorry,' he told her simply. 'Though perhaps what you've just told me helps me a little better to understand certain things about you.'

'What things?'

'Oh, things. Certain things that didn't add up.'

'And now they do?'

'They're beginning to.'

Camilla looked away, strangely disturbed by the suddenly profound look in his eyes—and by the illogical sense of satisfaction she had felt in unburdening herself to him. And though there was much more she could have told him, some instinct told her there was no need.

But suddenly the spell was broken as he asked her, 'So where does Eric fit into all this?'

'What do you mean, where does he fit in? I've already told you he's the man I'm going to marry!' For some inexplicable reason, the mention of Eric at that moment felt almost like an intrusion. 'What's this obsession with Eric, anyway? Why do you keep mentioning him?'

'Just curious, I guess.' He took another bite of his roll, leaned back in his seat and pushed back his sleeves. 'I know I've told you this before, but for the life of me I still can't figure out what a girl like you is doing with a guy like him.'

Which just went to prove how totally non-existent was this understanding he had just laid claim to! She felt both soothed and irritated by the revelation. Normality was restored, but something had been lost.

'Well, it makes sense to me,' she informed him curtly. 'Total sense. So, please don't worry yourself.'

He took a mouthful of his coffee and stretched his long legs out in front of him. 'Oh, I'm not worried, but I can't help wondering what the devil it is you see in him.'

There he was again, talking as though he knew Eric personally! Perhaps it was the lunacy of the whole situation that spurred her to offer a reply instead of just telling him to mind his own damned business. With perfect composure she took a bite of her roll. Let him not see how much he rattled her.

'As it happens, Eric and I have a great deal in common. We like the same sort of music. We enjoy doing the same sorts of things.' She chewed discreetly and carried on, deliberately avoiding Ross's gaze. The facetious mockery she would see there, she knew, would only put her off. 'What's more, our views on most things coincide. We have very similar outlooks on life. Our tastes are similar. We like the same things.' She paused and glanced across at him, satisfied with this assessment. 'I would say that Eric and I are a very highly compatible couple.'

The dark eyes scrutinised her face as, with a smile of satisfaction, she wound up her case. He seemed to be waiting for her to continue. 'Is that it?' he said at last.

The blue eyes sparked. 'What more do you want? Eric's a kind and decent man. He's going to make me an excellent husband!'

Thoughtfully, Ross narrowed his eyes, then, very slowly, he shook his head. 'You know, I seriously think you believe all that claptrap you've just told me.'

'Claptrap?'

'Claptrap,' he repeated. Then, in a gesture at once impatient and dismissive, he turned and tossed the crust of his bread roll over the guard rail into the sea. From out of nowhere, before it ever hit the water, a seagull swooped down to catch it in its bill, then wheeled away triumphantly to the squawking disapproval of it companions. Ross watched it go. 'The scavengers of the sea,' he observed. 'They'll accept anything that's edible.'

Camilla glared at the contemptuous dark profile, the strong, straight nose, the square, proud jaw, and felt the irritation bubbling inside her. A lesson in marine zoology was not what she was interested in right now. In a taut, even tone she demanded,'Would you mind explaining what you mean by claptrap?'

'Garbage. Nonsense. Utter baloney.' He raised one dark eyebrow and turned to look at her. 'All those reasons you gave me for marrying Eric. Claptrap, that's what they are.' Then, before she could intervene, he carried on, 'The world is full of

kind and decent people who share our opinions
and our taste in music. But, hell, that doesn't mean
to say we have to go and marry them!'

Camilla blinked at him, momentarily thrown by
the obvious logic of his argument. Then she
stiffened uneasily as, quite unexpectedly, he slid
along the bench towards her.

'There has to be more to it than that,' he told her.
'A very great deal more, I'd say.' An intense
expression filled his eyes as, catching her totally off
guard, he reached out one hand to grasp her arm.
'Does he move you when he's close, like this? Does
he feel like an extension of your soul?'

Camilla jerked involuntarily away as his
unexpected touch ignited her nerve-ends.
Indignantly, she met his gaze. 'And what is that
supposed to mean?' she shot back at him
defensively. If he was asking if Eric sparked in her
the raw sexual responses that she felt for him, then
her answer, without a shadow of a doubt had to be
no. But then, she reasoned, that was probably
because he had respected her wishes to keep their
courtship chaste—a chivalrous gesture of the type
that Ross McKeown would never understand!

She glared at him disapprovingly and charged,
'You're the one who's talking claptrap now! You
can make fun of me all you like, but I still claim
that a common outlook is important between two
people who intend to spend their lives together.
How can you expect to live in any kind of harmony
unless you agree about essential, basic things?'

'Oh, don't worry, I'm all for harmony, too.' He
smiled a blatantly disharmonious smile as he
dropped his hand from her arm at last and leaned

back, watching her beneath long lashes. 'But I don't think it's something two people can achieve through the sorts of superficialities you mentioned alone. What does it really matter if one partner likes Stravinsky and the other prefers Springsteen, or if one enjoys playing football and the other would rather stay at home and paint? Any relationship worth having should be strong enough to tolerate such differences.'

'Maybe,' she conceded reluctantly. The irrefutability of his reasoning was making her feel acutely uncomfortable. She decided, for a change, to put him on the spot. 'So, tell me, then, since you're the expert, what makes an ideal relationship?'

A self-mocking smile curled round his lips. He ran his fingers through his hair. 'Oh, I'm no expert,' he assured her. 'The ideal relationship, I'm afraid, is something that so far has eluded me.' His expression sobered. He looked straight at her. 'But I'll know beyond a shadow of a doubt if and when I ever find it—and it will have nothing whatsoever to do with compatibility of tastes in music.'

He was really rubbing that point in. 'Then what?' Camilla demanded caustically.

He shrugged broad shoulders and half turned away. 'It isn't easy to describe, but I know I'll recognise the girl for me, possibly without knowing anything about her. What I see in her eyes will be all I'll need to know. There'll be an instant bond, an instinctive understanding, that goes beyond all human calculation. And when we touch, or even when we don't, I'll feel as if she's a part of my soul.'

As he looked back at her Camilla looked away, aware that his words had struck a chord in her heart.

But an uneasy and faintly threatening chord. Though it surprised her to have to admit it, she had suddenly understood exactly what he meant.

Defensively, she raised her eyes. 'You're looking for a romantic ideal that only happens to the lucky few. Like most people, I'm sure, in the end you'll settle for less.'

'As you have, you mean?'

She had not meant that, though it was true. In spite of herself, she felt her face flame. 'I'm a realist,' she told him, glancing self-consciously down at her lap. 'I don't waste my time with impossible dreams.'

'And I'm an incurable romantic. I refuse to settle for anything less.'

As their eyes met, he was smiling, but behind the smile lay a deadly seriousness that Camilla could only wonder at—and, reluctantly, admire. He would have his dream or settle for nothing. She felt a twinge of envy at his resolve.

'So what happens if your dream girl doesn't come along? Do you intend to live your life alone?'

'If I have to,' he assured her. 'Though I thoroughly intend to treat myself to the occasional diversion along the way.'

That was more like it! Camilla thought at once. A bit of rough and ready pragmatism amid all the starry idealism! 'I take it by that that you intend to have affairs—or rather, that you do have affairs?' she corrected herself.

Ross smiled, amused by her boldness. 'Would you expect me to live like a monk?'

No, she would not expect that. A man like him, it would not be possible. As the old Laird had said, he would live life to the hilt.

'Perhaps you should consider a similar strategy yourself.' Ross was watching her now with a strange new expression. 'Instead of rushing into a second-rate marriage, indulge yourself in the occasional passing fancy until that special someone comes along.'

What was he saying? Camilla blinked at him, her skin growing suddenly uncomfortably warm at the invitation he seemed to have implied. Was it merely her imagination, or had his suggestion had a personal ring? She felt herself stiffen. 'No, thank you,' she replied. 'That may suit you, but it would never suit me. And besides,' she reminded him sharply, 'you forget, I've already found my special someone.'

As he nodded—'Yes, of course, I forgot'—she turned her gaze deliberately seawards, pointedly ending the conversation. She would not listen to this disruptive talk. She had chosen the path she intended to follow and she would not be diverted from it. Eric was not, and never would be, the romantic soulmate that Ross had spoken of, but he was a good man for all that and she would be lucky to have him for a husband.

She glanced up at the swooping, diving seagulls, still following the ferry as it headed for the islands. Let Ross, if he happened to feel so inclined, go chasing after impossible dreams. She, for her part, in her short lifetime, had had enough of struggle and uncertainty. What she needed now were simple love and security and those were precisely the things that Eric offered her.

He was the best future she was ever likely to have,

and she intended hanging on to him.

They finally reached the Isle of Mhoire just as the sun was going down. By then, they were the only two passengers left on the ferry, all the others having disembarked at the various islands along the way.

As they climbed into the Land Rover and trundled down the ramp on to dry land, the ferryman stood and waved them off. 'Wednesday, eight a.m. sharp, remember!' he called after them. 'That's our next sailing time back to the mainland. Be sure you're here in plenty of time!'

Don't worry, Camilla assured him silently. I'll be the first person in the queue! She had a feeling that by eight a.m. on Wednesday she'd be ready to swim back under her own steam!

She leaned back in her seat and looked out at the view, at the rugged mountains inland and the perfectly stretching sandy shore, all bathed now in the fiery, crimson-red rays of a spectacularly setting sun. It was all so peaceful, so untouched, like some secret little corner of a private paradise. As ever, there was only one discordant note. She turned in her seat and glanced across at him.

'How far to our hotel?' she asked. 'I could do with something to eat.'

'Hotel?' He turned to look at her, a look of amusement his face. 'I'm afraid, on this little island, the first hotel has still to be built.'

Irritation flared inside her. He took such pleasure in telling her she was wrong! 'Boarding house, then. Bed and breakfast. Wherever it is we're going to spend the night.'

'I'm afraid there are no boarding houses or bed and breakfasts, either. They don't have very much call for such things over here.'

'So where are we going to sleep? Under the stars, on a bed of heather?'

'If that's what you'd like, I'm sure we could arrange it.' He held her eyes for a moment, mockingly. 'Don't tell me that, after all, this is a sign that a hint of romance lurks in that cold, calculating soul of yours?'

Cold and calculating—was that how he thought of her? If it was it just showed how little he understood. Oddly hurt, she turned her attention to the road, refusing to dignify his mockery with an answer. Wherever he was taking her, she would find out soon enough.

The sun had dipped beyond the horizon when they drew up at last outside a pretty whitewashed farmhouse, nestling in a quiet corner of the valley. 'This is it,' Ross informed her. 'Come and meet Davie and Katharine McLeod, your hosts for the night.'

A moment or two later, in answer to his knock, the door was opened by an apple-cheeked young woman with two small children clinging to her skirts. At the sight of Ross, her face blossomed in smiles. She threw her arms around his neck. 'Ross McKeown! Well, of all the surprises! Come in, come in! It's grand to see you!'

As they were ushered into a narrow hallway, Ross quickly introduced Camilla. Katharine McLeod shook her hand warmly and smiled at her with bright hazel eyes. 'A welcome to you, my dear. Any friend of Ross's is more than welcome in this house.'

Through in the parlour, her husband Davie was seated by the fire, three more children of varying ages gathered around his knee. At the sight of Ross he laid down the storybook that he had evidently been reading from and rose from his seat, one hand held out, grinning as widely as his wife. 'Ross, man, you're just in time! Kate's got supper cooking on the stove.'

Camilla couldn't help but feel gratefully impressed as, half an hour or so later, she and Ross and Davie and Katharine seated themselves round a laden table while the children played quietly by the fire. She had barely been introduced to these people and already she had been made to feel like an old friend.

She dug into her delicious lamb stew and glanced across with mixed feelings at Ross. The McLeods evidently doted on him and were honoured and delighted to have him as their guest. But perhaps the most astonishing thing of all was that 'Uncle Ross', as the children called him, seemed to fit so naturally into this homely milieu. Without outwardly seeming to change an atom, this wild and unpredictable man was suddenly a part of this big, warm family.

Eventually the conversation got round to what had brought Ross and Camilla to the island. Davie and Katharine exchanged glances, then Davie confided to Ross, 'I heard tell there was a stranger on the island just the other day. A young lad in his twenties, by all accounts—though we didn't set eyes on him ourselves.'

As Ross frowned, seeming to consider this intelligence, Katharine laid a hand on Camilla's arm. 'In a small place like this a stranger gets noticed and word quickly gets around.' She smiled at her young guest. 'Nobody means any harm by it. They're just curious, that's all.' She turned to look at Ross across the table. 'If this stranger had anything to do with the disappearance of the *Ceò do dh'òr*, or the bringing of it here, I'm sure you'll find out soon enough.'

But it was already late and their investigations had to wait until the following morning. After the children were tucked up in bed, the four adults gathered round the fire for a cup of coffee and some quiet chat, then, diplomatically, Ross rose to his feet.

'I think it's time we all turned in. I know it's long past Kate's and Davie's bedtime.' He threw Camilla a knowing wink. 'I happen to know that these good people have been up and busy since the crack of dawn, and they'll be up again at the same time tomorrow. They're both far too polite to say it, but they're falling asleep before our eyes.'

'Ross McKeown, you're quite incorrigible!' With a good-natured cluck of reproof, Katharine waved a finger at Ross. 'How dare you suggest to Camilla that Davie and I are unwilling hosts?'

As she got to her feet to stand beside him, Ross affectionately took her arm. 'Not unwilling,' he assured her. 'Never unwilling. Just tired.'

Katharine giggled and stifled a yawn. 'Well, now you come to mention it . . . maybe it is time we all turned in.' She glanced up at the tall dark man at her side. 'Will the but'n'ben be all right? As you know, we've no spare beds here. Too many children. I'm afraid.' She giggled again and threw a smile at her husband. 'That's what happens when you've no television.'

The but'n'ben turned out to be a small converted outhouse at the back of the cottage. 'Some of the farmhands use it when we're extra busy—like at harvest time,' Katharine explained to Camilla as, torch in hand, she escorted her guests across the courtyard. 'I'll leave you, Ross, to settle the pair of you in.' She smiled at Camilla as she handed over the key. 'He's stayed here many times before.'

Inside, there were two rooms, tiny, warm and immaculate, and a bathroom with a shower unit. 'You can have the bedroom,' Ross told her, as she eyed with a sudden flare of trepidation the pair of comfortable-looking twin beds. He followed her eyes and smiled a slow smile. 'I'll sleep on the put-you-up next door.'

Relief rushed through her. 'Fine,' she said.

'Unless, of course,' he added silkily, deliberately holding her eyes, 'you fancy a bit of company?'

'I do not,' she assured him, much too quickly. 'Thank you, all the same.' Her eyes slid anxiously to the bedroom door, surreptitiously checking that there was a key in the lock. Observing that there was, she breathed with relief. She would start to feel a great deal happier once he was locked on the other side!

But, for once, he was behaving like a gentleman, retreating discreetly while she unpacked her things, even allowing her first use of the bathroom. Evidently, she thought to herself, with a measure of quiet satisfaction, the presence of Katharine and Davie in the cottage just across the way was having a pleasantly chastening effect.

After her shower she had changed into a pair of

cotton pyjamas and matching blue-striped robe, which she had wrapped extra decorously around her slim form, the belt secured tightly at her waist. Now she sat on the edge of her bed, listening to the sounds of the splashing shower coming from the adjoining bathroom. She stretched her legs and stifled a yawn. 'Hurry,' she murmured to the bathroom door. 'I want to get into bed and get some sleep.'

A moment later, as though in answer to her plea, the shower was switched off and the lock shot back. Then she felt her heart give an odd little lurch as Ross came striding out of the bathroom, dressed only in jeans, naked to the waist.

He paused to look at her, his powerful frame suddenly seeming to completely fill the tiny space between the bathroom and the bed, a tall and vibrantly masculine figure, the dark-skinned planes of his shoulders and chest broad and taut and muscular. A slow smile lit deep in his eyes. 'I wonder if you would do me a favour?' he said.

'A favour?' All at once, at the devilish look in his eyes, a spasm of anxiety went rushing through her, fixing her motionless to the bed. She met his gaze with an effort. 'What sort of favour?' she croaked.

In answer, he half turned round so that she could see his damaged shoulder. 'That dressing Doc Fraser put on for me, I'm afraid it got wet and came off in the shower.' He glanced appealingly over his shoulder. 'I wonder if you could just stick it back on for me?'

Instantly Camilla was on her feet, a frown of concern puckering her face, all her anxiety instantly forgotten, as she crossed over to investigate. 'Really, you should have been more careful,' she clucked admonishingly at him, observing with some relief that only a corner of the dressing was undone. With gentle fingers she smoothed it back into place. 'Didn't the doctor tell you you're not supposed to get it wet?'

'Yes, Nurse.' He was smiling as he turned round, a wicked, humorous, taunting smile, and Camilla's temporarily vanished anxiety came rushing back in on her with full force.

Somehow she had managed to wedge herself in a tiny corner beside the door, hemmed in on every side, it seemed, by Ross's massive, looming frame. And she was virtually pressed up against him. She could smell his heady, masculine scent, feel his pulsing animal warmth. She shuddered, her limbs suddenly stricken, unable to move. All at once, she could scarcely breathe. Her heart felt as big as a football in her chest.

'Thank you.' He hadn't moved and she couldn't find the words to ask him to. He looked down at her with those fierce grey eyes, their expression momentarily softened. 'You know, when you drop your iron lady act, you're really quite a decent human being. You should make a point of dropping it more often.'

Camilla swallowed and attempted a glare. 'I've fixed your dressing,' she told him tightly. Then added, unwisely, 'Will that be all?'

Predictably, he shook his dark head. 'Since you ask, Camilla, there's just one more thing.'

At least she had the wit not to ask what it was. She had no need. She had already guessed. As he continued, motionless, to gaze down at her, she felt her whole body tense. Then a sudden bright spark of excitement flared as he leaned towards her.

Softly, one hand was circling her waist, making the breath freeze in her throat, while the other reached out to touch her hair, then slid round slowly to the back of her neck.

She could have pulled away. She had ample time. But, instead, to her own quiet horror, she closed her eyes and waited, breathless and helpless in his arms, to feel the intoxicating brush of his lips.

When it came, her heart seemed to burst into flames. Deep inside her she shuddered and moaned. Beyond her control, her body clung to him, a fierce, dark longing invading her loins.

The mouth pressed to hers was hot and urgent, prising her trembling lips apart, and the hand that swept round to cover her breast moved hungrily over her aching flesh.

Only half believing that she could really be allowing this to happen, that she was a willing and eager collaborator, Camilla shuddered with helpless pleasure as, in one bold and breathless movement, he snatched the robe and the pyjama jacket open to gain greedy access to her naked breasts.

Then, fiercely, he was caressing her, drawing her nipples into hard, tight peaks beneath his fingers, and she was pressing herself wantonly against him as she felt her whole body stir with sinful pleasure.

With a moan she let her fingers trace the warm, hard shoulders, then reach to tangle in his hair as his lips hungrily devoured her, igniting in her a savage agony of wanting far more powerful than her will to resist.

But then, abruptly, he loosened his embrace and

paused for a moment to look down into her eyes, consuming her with that burning dark gaze. Only half comprehending, she looked back at him as, unsteadily, he took a step back, relief and regret fuddling her brain as he told her in a low, rough voice, 'I think I'd better say goodnight, Camilla, before things get totally out of hand.'

Then, before she could answer him, he turned and strode into the other room.

After the door closed behind him, Camilla sat down, struggling to gather her shattered poise. Her body still burned, her limbs were trembling, her brain was swimming inside her head. What had just happened was quite appalling. She thought of Eric and closed her eyes. Appalling, she repeated to herself. How could she ever have allowed it to occur?

She lay on the bed and curled into a ball, tears of shame and resentment pricking her eyes. Somehow he had tricked her into reacting as she had. Like the savage that she knew he was, he had cast some wicked spell on her.

Like a dog with a bone, she clung to that thought as, still trembling, she slipped beneath the covers at last. 'I hate you, Ross McKeown! I hate you!' she kept muttering over and over to herself—yet knowing with a growing sense of desolation that it simply was no longer true.

CHAPTER SEVEN

NEXT morning Camilla and Ross were up with the lark, taking turns to shower and dress in the bathroom, with never a reference to last night. Evidently they were both agreed that it was a foolish lapse, best forgotten.

By the time they crossed over to the farmhouse, looking for breakfast, Davie was already out in the fields and Katharine was down in the back garden, hanging a gargantuan load of washing on the line, while three of her boisterous brood played cops and robbers among the chickens. At the sight of her two guests she immediately abandoned her task and, beaming, ushered them into her kitchen.

'Sit you down,' she commanded. 'I'll make you fresh porridge and toast.'

And there was no arguing with her, either. As Camilla started to protest that there was no need for Katharine to put herself out, that she was perfectly capable of preparing breakfast for Ross and herself, Kate waved her protestations aside. 'If you want to make yourself useful,' she smiled, 'you can keep an eye on the bairns for me.'

Ross was already doing a good job of that. The two smallest of the youngsters, Robbie and baby Kirsty, had followed the grown-ups indoors and were now clustering excitedly around 'Uncle Ross', chattering and laughing and vying for his attention as he lifted Kirsty on to his knee.

As Katharine busied herself at the Aga at the far end of the kitchen, Camilla watched the scene with interest, greatly impressed, as she had been last night, by how totally at ease Ross appeared to be with the children. And they with him. Impressed, too, by the way he seemed to become almost like a different person in their company. Relaxed and gentle, of infinite patience, so unlike his usual self.

Dressed in his customary jeans and, today, a plain black roll-neck sweater that echoed the darkness of his hair and brought into dramatic sharp relief the strong, handsome lines of his deeply tanned face, Ross's tall, powerful, ultra-masculine frame, that could at times appear almost threatening, seemed miraculously transformed into the guise of gentle protector. It was a role, she knew instinctively, that he would perform both diligently and well. He would be as fierce and unrelenting in defence of those he cared about as he was capable of being when he chose to attack.

The thought brought an unexpected tightness to the back of Camilla's throat. The enemies of Ross McKeown had reason to lie sleepless in their beds, but blessed indeed would be those he loved. For a fleeting second she felt a shaft of regret that she would never know such a privilege—and a flash of envy for the girl who one day would. Then, suddenly feeling his eyes on her, she glanced away, hot with confusion.

'So, what do you think? Will I make a good father?' With almost uncanny precision he had read into her thoughts again. Smiling, he gently loosened the little girl's embrace around his neck and went on to enlighten Camilla, 'I intend having quite a brood myself. At least as many as Davie and Kate.'

'Always supposing, of course, that you manage to find that ideal love of yours!' There was a hint of resentment in Camilla's voice as she shot the challenge across at him. She resented his calm assumptions regarding his own future—but, much more, she resented the way he had made her feel.

'Oh, I shall find her. Have no fear about that.' He narrowed his grey eyes momentarily and, suddenly serious, looked her straight in the face. 'In spite of what I said before, I don't really plan to spend my life alone. So I have to find her. Remember, unlike you, I shall settle for nothing less.'

Camilla let her gaze slide away, wincing beneath the bitter bite of his words. What could he, who had been brought up to believe that his every desire was attainable, possibly begin to understand of the need to make do and compromise? In her struggle out of the mire she had learned not to set her sights too high. She flicked an angry glance across at him. Not everyone could hold out for what they desired. Some simply had to settle for what they needed.

He caught her glance and held it, his dark eyes taunting. 'No doubt you and Eric plan on conforming to the regulation two point two offspring once you're married? Eric definitely wouldn't want any more than that.'

Suddenly genuinely at a loss for an answer, Camilla observed with a sense of relief that

Katharine was bearing down on them with two large, steaming plates. Beaming that luminous smile that seemed to hover constantly round her lips, she laid the plates down in front of her guests. 'Good Highland porridge. There's nothing to beat it,' she announced, pushing a jug of fresh milk towards them and drawing up a chair. 'And now, I'll join you for a cup of coffee before I get on with my chores.'

The porridge was delicious, creamy and smooth, and a million light years away from the tasteless instant variety that was all Camilla had ever known. She put her head down and ate, grateful for the distraction, and tried to shut out the niggling revelation that Ross's remark had brought home to her.

The truth was that she and Eric had never discussed their views on children, nor ever once raised the subject of how many they would have. For the very first time that struck her as odd—though, she told herself firmly, it was a meaningless omission. They had plenty of time to discuss such matters and, she felt sure, Eric's views would coincide with her own.

It was simply irritating to discover that, while she was ignorant of the views of her future fiancé, she was now fully apprised of, and in perfect concord with, those of the arrogant Ross McKeown!

After breakfast they set out on their search.

'I suggest we start off at the old keep where the jewels used to be kept. If this benevolent thief you so firmly believe in really does exist, it seems the most logical place for him to have put them.'

Camilla could find no fault with his logic, though she knew he only half-believed in her theory. 'Let's go, then,' she agreed, as she hoisted her camera-bag into the back of the Land Rover and climbed into the passenger seat. The sooner they got started, the sooner they would be done—and the sooner they would be able to return to the mainland and end this uneasy alliance of theirs.

The old keep was on the other side of the island and Ross took the rocky coast-road, past spectacular beaches and cliffs, following the inland curves of the hills, purple with heather. Camilla gazed out at the unfolding scenery, then darted a secret glance at the man at her side. What must it feel like, she wondered, to know that one would one day inherit all of this, not to mention Castle Crannach and the enormous estate that went with it as well? To be so securely rooted in, and such an essential part of, the historical continuum of life? Perhaps, in one who knew so securely his unequivocal place in the scheme of things, a little arrogance could sometimes be forgiven.

With a little wistful sigh of understanding she turned her attention back to the road. It was strange. In spite of their almost constant squabbling there was a growing sense of ease between them—like the unexpected sense of warm familiarity she had come to feel for this wild place.

Yet both the place and the man, in spite of their strange pull on her, possessed a danger she was growing increasingly aware of. They posed too many questions she could not answer and threatened to strike at the very foundations of everything she had ever believed in.

After three hours' meticulous search through the semi-ruined clifftop keep, it was beginning to look as though their trip to the island had been a waste of time. They had been through every one of the rooms, hunting through every nook and cranny, but there was no sign of the *Ceò do dh'òr*.

Still Camilla remained unshakeable in her belief that it was there. 'It *has* to be,' she insisted, not caring how irrational she sounded. 'There's no other explanation for the way you escaped with your life from that accident.'

Ross shrugged indulgently, hiding his scepticism. 'So, let's go on looking, if you're so sure.'

Half an hour later, they were glad they had.

It was Camilla who had the first suspicion of success. Having searched in all the obvious places, like cupboards and fireplaces and under stairs, she had decided to look in some less likely, and less salubrious spots. Like the old open drains, long dried up, that ran from the kitchens to a ditch outside. With an effort, she had removed the heavy iron grille and was crouching down on the flagstone floor, reaching down into the darkness where her eyes could not see.

At first her fingers waved emptily in the air. There appeared to be nothing there. Determinedly, she stretched a little further. It was as though something was telling her this was the place. Then a moment later her heart nearly stopped as her fingers made contact with something solid. It felt like a box, she thought with rising excitement, but, as she stretched further, struggling to grasp it with her fingers, infuriatingly it slid further away.

She leapt to her feet. 'Ross! Ross! Come quickly!' she called. 'I think I've found them! I think they're here!'

Instantly, he appeared from the next room. 'Where? he demanded.

'In there!' Camilla pointed at the open drain, her face alive with anticipation. 'I felt something, but I couldn't get a grip on it. I couldn't quite reach. My arm wasn't long enough.'

'Let me.' At once he was down on his knees, bending over the open drain, one sleeve of his black cashmere sweater pushed back as he stretched his long, muscular arm inside. Camilla stood over him, anxiously watching, feeling the silence almost unbearable as she waited for his response. Then his face broke into a slow, soft smile. He nodded. 'I think you're right.'

The next moment, with a bit of delicate manoeuvring, he lifted the object from the gaping drain. It was covered in dust, but instantly recognisable as the little carved wooden box that contained the *Ceò do dh'òr*. Or had. Her heart in her mouth, Camilla watched as, rising slowly to his feet, Ross carefully turned the silver key. Without a word, he lifted the lid, then turned the box round for her to see. And there, on their bed of deep blue velvet, unharmed, lay the precious jewels.

'I knew it!' She could have jumped for joy. She wanted to throw her arms around his neck. Her blue eyes sparkled with happy triumph.

'Somehow, I just *knew* they were here!'

Ross was grinning from ear to ear, evidently as thrilled as she. 'I suppose that's what they mean by woman's intuition. I'm glad that, for once, I paid it heed.' The dark grey eyes sought hers then held them for a moment. 'Thanks, Camilla,' he offered sincerely. 'I don't mind saying that if it hadn't been for you I would never have thought of looking here.'

'But how did they get here? Who brought them? We still don't know that. Or why.' Camilla's smile broke into a frown. 'It must have been that young man that Davie spoke about. But who on earth could he have been?'

Ross shook his head and smiled at her, as, carefully, he closed the box. 'Right now I'm not naming any names, but let's just say I have my suspicions. We'll find out if I'm right all in good time. The important thing is, we've got the jewels back—and the one I have to thank is you.'

He paused, the dark eyes scanning her face, then, taking her totally by surprise, he stepped towards her suddenly and caught her jaw in the cup of his hand. The grey eyes twinkled into hers. 'Accept this as a token of my gratitude,' he murmured with a smile as, deliberately and quite unhurriedly, he reached down to plant a kiss on her lips.

It was quite the nicest kiss she had ever received. Soft and warm and gently lingering. But its gentleness concealed a fiery sensuality that, quite literally, took her breath away. As his fingers slid round to the back of her head, trailing through the silky strands of hair, she felt the blood grow warm in her veins and her heart begin to beat against her ribs.

Then, as his lips grew firm and moved against hers and the warmth of his hard male body pressed close, she closed her eyes, with a little sigh, lost in the sweetness of the moment. For somehow, here and now, this shared kiss between them seemed like the most natural thing in the world.

As they drew apart, he looked down at her tenderly. 'I suggest you do your photographs while we're here. We're leaving the island tomorrow, remember. You won't get another opportunity to photograph the *Ceò do dh'òr* in its original setting.'

Camilla nodded. 'I was thinking the same.' Though that was not really strictly true, she admitted with a secret smile to herself, as she went off to collect her camera-bag. What she had really been thinking was that she wished that kiss could go on forever!

The light and the setting were perfect. These photographs promised to be quite spectacular, Camilla realised with quiet pleasure as, up on the battlements of the old keep, she shot roll after roll of film. They would definitely be the high spot of the book. Quite possibly the high spot of her whole career.

From a discreet distance, Ross watched, his grey eyes filled with fascination as he observed the intent, graceful movements of the blonde-haired girl. Camilla could feel his eyes on her, but for once the dark gaze didn't bother her. Oddly, she found his presence soothing, even encouraging, in a way. Strange, she found herself thinking in passing. Usually, when she was working, she disliked an audience.

It was well after lunchtime by the time she had finished. Ross glanced at his watch as she packed her cameras away. 'I suggest we go back to Kate and Davie's now and see if we can rustle up some lunch. I don't know about you, but I could eat a horse.'

'Me too,' Camilla agreed. Then she giggled and met his eyes. 'Let's just keep our fingers crossed that Kate's got a couple of horses in the freezer.'

'If she hasn't, we'll send her down to the supermarket to buy some.' Ross was smiling, holding her eyes. Then, as she started to swing the camera-bag over her shoulder, he reached out and caught it with his hand. 'I'll carry this,' he insisted. 'It's far too heavy for you.'

At the brush of his fingers against her arm, Camilla felt an involuntary shiver, and the oddly intense look in his eyes sent fingers of excitement down her spine. Still, she managed to look back at him levelly. 'There's really no need, you know. I carry it about all the time.'

He swung the bag easily over his shoulder, tucking the *Ceò do dh'òr* box under his arm. 'Not today you don't, young lady.' His free hand went round her shoulder as he led her across the battlements towards the stone stairs. 'Today you're going to be given the royal treatment. It's no more than you deserve.'

Camilla smiled to herself. Such a display of chivalry—so unexpected and, frankly, so pleasing! Enjoy it while you can, she told herself wryly. This good humour of his may not last.

In that prediction she was to be proved right.

though she could never have guessed how his humour would change.

It was as they were climbing into the car, her camera-bag and the *Ceò do dh'òr* stowed away in the back, that a sudden thought occurred to her. 'What are you going to do with the jewels now that you've found them again?' she asked.

He revved the engine and slipped into first. 'Why, I'm taking them back to Castle Crannach, of course.'

It was not the answer she had been expecting and, quite frankly, it appalled her. 'But how can you think of doing that after what almost happened?'

He glanced across to meet her eyes. 'What happened, Camilla, was coincidence. I told you before, I don't believe in curses and still don't believe in them now.'

'But why take the chance?' she insisted, aware that his answer bothered her perhaps more than it should. 'Why not leave the jewels in some safe place on the island? You don't need to have them at the castle.'

'I want them at the castle, and that's where they're going.' There was a sudden impatient edge to his tone. 'They've been kept at the castle since long before I was born. I can see no reason to change that now.'

'But look at what happened to your father! Do you want the same thing to happen to you? At least leave them on the island till your thirty-fifth birthday. Surely a few months wouldn't do any harm!'

This time he did not look at her, though she

could see his irritation in the set of his jaw. 'You're wasting your breath, Camilla. Just drop the subject. Please.'

But she could not. He was putting himself in pointless danger and, somehow, she had to make him see sense. To his silent annoyance, she was still arguing her case as they drew up outside the McLeod farmhouse.

There appeared to be no one at home. Katharine had evidently taken the kids and gone out. Stiff-legged, Ross led the way round to the but'n'ben at the back. 'We'll just drop off your bag and the jewels, then see about fixing ourselves something to eat.'

Camilla followed him, seething with frustration. She had the distinct impression that throughout the latter part of their journey he hadn't been listening to a word she'd said. As he laid down her bag and locked the *Ceò do dh'òr* in a cupboard in a corner of the room, she remained standing in the doorway, glaring at his tall, impassive frame.

Angrily, she addressed his broad back. 'Are you always so damned pig-headed about everything? Don't you ever listen to anyone's opinion but your own?'

He turned and looked through her, heading for the door. 'I'm hungry, Camilla. Let's go and eat.'

But as he made to come past her she stood her ground in the doorway, like a mouse attempting to block the path of a lion. 'Why do you have to be so damned stubborn? Can't you see it's for your own good?'

He was standing over her, the dark eyes like lasers. 'Camilla, kindly let me past. I'm starting to get sick and tired of all this nonsense.'

His attitude was infuriatingly condescending, as though he were dealing with a blameless but tiresome child. And his next move, she anticipated, would be to gently but firmly remove her from the doorway, like some inanimate object that had got in his way. Angry resentment welled up inside her. She would not simply be brushed aside! On a sudden impulse, she raised her fists and began to beat her forearms against his chest.

'Damn you, Ross McKeown!' she shrilled. 'Won't you listen to what I'm trying to say?'

He caught her wrists and held them securely. 'My dear Camilla, I've already listened enough. And I can assure you that physical violence isn't going to succeed where irrational argument has already failed.' He paused for a moment, looking down at her, and, through the irritation of before, another emotion seemed to flicker in his face. 'As I said, I suggest we forget all this nonsense and go and fix ourselves something to eat.'

'But it's not nonsense!' She struggled to free herself. 'How can you be so sure?'

Still he held her. 'It *is* nonsense, Camilla. Your concern, though flattering, is misplaced.'

As he looked down into her eyes, she glanced away, suddenly embarrassed and confused by the depth of that concern. Defensively, she told him in a quiet murmur, 'I just think you're being foolish, that's all.'

'Foolish? You may be right.' He continued to look down at her, still holding her lightly by the wrists, and again there was a flash of that other emotion deep down in his eyes. He smiled strangely and leaned towards her. 'And tell me about this, Camilla. Is this foolish, too?'

Then there was a moment, a long, endless moment, before his lips came down to cover hers.

As his mouth claimed hers, he released her wrists so that she was free to escape if she wished. But instead, as his arms slid round her waist, drawing her more firmly against him, Camilla felt her body melt against him, hungry for his touch.

His kiss, at first, was soft and gentle, a teasing whisper of sensation. Yet Camilla was instantly aroused, sweet shivers of longing sweeping through her. Then the pressure of his mouth grew firm and hungry, and she could feel the passion rise in him as he prised her trembling lips apart and entered her sweetness with his tongue.

A shudder went through her then as, already half inebriated with the conquering heat of his mouth on hers, she felt his hand push beneath her sweater and slide upwards to cup her breast. In one impatient movement he had pushed the lacy bra aside, so that the swollen firmness of her breast fell naked and eager into his hand.

His body was hard against her own, making her moan with growing anguish, then she gasped aloud as with wicked precision his fingers squeezed the tight, hard nipple.

That was the moment, she realised later, as a sweet, sharp ecstasy went shooting through her and an urgent longing gripped her soul, that she knew in her heart that there was no turning back. The wild emotions that ravaged her senses could not be tamed and pushed aside. It was too late for that. She was in their thrall. As with a human cannonball being shot out of a cannon, the touch-paper of her desire had been ignited and she had crossed the point of no return.

Ross seemed to sense the half-conscious decision. He drew back for a moment and looked into her face. 'Are you sure, Camilla?' he asked.

She nodded and leaned against him, longing to feel the naked touch of his flesh. 'Absolutely sure,' she confirmed resolutely. She had never felt more sure of anything in her life.

Without another word, then, he led her through to the other room and the bed where she had slept alone last night. Now, with a sigh, she let him lay her down, his fingers caressing her hair, her face, as he began to peel her clothes away. And she, compliant and eager, shrugging impatiently out of the thick grey sweater, wriggling free from the restricting grey wool trousers. She could not be rid of them quickly enough.

How odd, she thought fleetingly, mildly bemused, as her underclothes joined the heap on the floor, that this should all happen so easily, so naturally, when I have never been naked with a man before.

Then he was lying alongside her, his hard, naked body pressed close to her own, and she could feel her senses singing as his warm lips pressed kisses against her flesh. He kissed her temples, her cheek, her chin, the warm, scented hollow of her throat, then swept round to her shoulder and back to her earlobe, making her sigh and shiver deliciously as he nuzzled against the crook of her neck.

'My sweet thing,' he murmured against her ear,

his voice low and grainy, thick with the need in him. 'Finally, you're going to be mine.'

His hands swept urgently over her flesh, her shoulders, her neck, the dip of her waist, pausing to caress the curve of her belly before scooping upwards to claim her breasts.

Camilla gasped with fierce, sweet pleasure as his palms brushed the pink, erect peaks of her nipples, making the blood burn in her loins and her body tremble and arch against him. Instinctively her own hands reached for him, boldly, without inhibition, her fingers tracing the broad, muscular shoulders, the hard, flat planes of his belly and chest, matching caress for caress, pleasure for pleasure.

'Oh, Camilla, I want you. I want you so badly.'

Hotly, burningly, his lips moved over her, her throat, her collarbone, her shoulders, her breasts, then she gasped, sensation exploding right through her, as he paused to draw one nipple into his mouth. The pleasure was excruciating as he tugged hungrily at the aroused, aching flesh, his tongue flickering wickedly, like a serpent's, making her moan deep in her throat.

'Ross! Ross!' She had never burned like this before, never longed so desperately for any man. Nor known before that any man could respond so passionately to her.

When at last he came to her, their bodies seemed to slip together like silk. At once, her heart and her body were filled with him. With his power, his passion, his fierceness, his strength.

And through the agony and the ecstasy of this joining of their bodies, as he carried her on magic

wings towards release, in one secret, barely
conscious corner of her mind, wonderingly,
half-disbelievingly, it occurred to Camilla in a
flash of pure joy that this was how she had always
dreamed it would be, yet never really dared to
hope.

Next morning Ross and Camilla were down at the
little jetty, waiting for the ferry, in plenty of time.
They had not spoken a civil word to each other
since they had left the McLeods'. The air between
them was electric.

Resolutely Camilla stared straight ahead,
avoiding even a flicker of a glance in Ross's
direction as they drove up the narrow metal ramp
and parked the Land Rover on the port side of the
ferry. She longed desperately for this voyage to be
over, to be back in safe seclusion at the Stag Hotel,
with Ross out of sight and, hopefully, out of mind
up at Castle Crannach.

Her heart ached with a pain she could not even
define—yet which was fierce and numbing, for all
that. The magic between them that had flared so
unexpectedly had turned to bitter cinders long
before nightfall.

For one thing, despite her pleas, Ross had
remained immovable on the question of the *Ceò
do dh'òr*. In callous disregard of her protestations,
it was with them now, in the car, on its way back
to Castle Crannach. But that particular difference
of opinion, hotly disputed though it had been, was
not the real reason that she had gone to bed with
the taste of bitter bile in her mouth.

Camilla felt her stomach tighten, remembering

what had passed between them last night, and put up a silent prayer that, for the remainder of the journey, the subject would not be raised again. But, as she had feared, her prayer fell unheard.

They had almost reached Gairloch on the mainland and were standing uneasily together by the guard rail, ostensibly looking out to sea, when suddenly, in a cool, hard tone, Ross remarked without preamble, 'So that's the end of that, I take it?'

His words were like a skewer driving into her heart. Yesterday, when they had made love, had felt like a beginning that could never end. But, in a cool tone, that masked the pain in her soul, she answered now without a quaver, 'I told you, what happened was a foolish mistake. I lost my head. I didn't know what I was doing.' With difficulty, she focused on the hard grey eyes. 'So, as I told you before, you're fooling yourself if you think for one minute that there'll be any repetition.'

She had made that clear to him last night when he had so shamelessly tried to talk her into an affair, wounding her terribly and bursting the bubble between them. Yet the expression that now shone from his eyes was as cool and unrepentant as it had been then.

'So, you didn't know what you were doing? I rather got the impression you did. Never mind.' His gaze twisted sharply. 'At least now you'll have a real experience to compare with all those passionless nights that lie ahead for you with Eric.'

His harsh words fell upon her like a curse, and her heart seemed to shrink with the chill wind of their truth. Yesterday would live for ever inside her, a constant pain, an unforgettable pleasure. Yet, defensively, vindictively, she heard herself answer, 'Don't flatter yourself! I've practically forgotten yesterday already.'

In stony silence they drove up to the castle, a wall like a glacier rising between them, both totally unprepared for the latest surprise that fate had waiting in store for them.

For, standing on the castle steps, looking incongruous in a grey City suit, waiting for them, stood Eric.

CHAPTER EIGHT

'ERIC, darling! What a wonderful surprise!'

Instantly, Camilla was sprinting across the gravelled forecourt towards the slim, fair figure in the pinstripe suit. With a cry of surprise she threw her arms around his neck, feeling a warm, sharp surge of relief sweep through her. All at once, miraculously, order had been restored in a world grown chaotic.

Eric hugged her, affection and concern in his good-natured face. 'Camilla, darling, I was worried about you. I didn't know where the hell you were. I got this garbled message from my secretary. I hope you don't mind me just turning up?'

'Of course I don't! I'm delighted to see you.' Like a shipwreck survivor clinging to a life raft, Camilla held on tightly to his arm. 'We had to go to the Isle of Mhoire in search of the missing *Ceò do dh'òr.*' She smiled as he frowned, uncomprehending. 'Don't worry, I'll explain everything as soon as we get back to the hotel.' Impatiently, she started to tug at his sleeve. 'Come on, let's go back now. I'm dying to talk to you.'

But, gently, Eric held her back. He slipped an arm around her waist and admonished her softly with a smile. 'Just a minute, darling. You're forgetting something,' he chided. 'I think it would only be polite if you were to introduce me to this gentleman first.'

He was nodding politely in the direction of Ross, who had remained standing by the side of the Land Rover, hips leaning lightly against the bonnet, strong arms folded across his chest.

Ross looked back at them with an unfathomable expression, part aloof, superior detachment, part some indefinable, darker emotion that, deep in her soul, made Camilla shiver. He straightened now and took a step towards Eric, one hand extended, and smiled politely.

'Ross McKeown,' he supplied in a cool tone. 'I'm very pleased to meet you, Eric.' As the two men shook hands, briefly, Camilla continued to cling to Eric, eyes uneasily downcast, not quite daring to look straight at Ross. Suddenly, she was all too aware of how vulnerable his presence made her. What if, out of malice, he were to make some revealing remark to Eric about what had happened yesterday? She held her breath as he continued, 'I hope you didn't mind me spiriting your fianceé off to the Western Isles for a couple of days?' Sardonic amusement snaked round his lips. He paused for a moment, then went on, 'However, as you can see, I've brought her back to you all in one piece.'

The dark eyes slid across to Camilla, making her flush beneath the laserlike gaze. 'I'll leave her to explain what we were up to. Quite an exciting little tale.'

As he turned away, Camilla breathed again. Nervously, she squeezed Eric's arm. 'Come on. Let's go,' she urged, and nodded in the direction of the little hire car, parked now, she was relieved to see, ready and waiting in a corner of the forecourt. 'Let's go straight back to the hotel.'

They were half way to the car when, across the forecourt, Ross's voice came booming out. 'Hang on just a minute! Haven't you forgotten something?'

Camilla whirled round, her heart beating faster. What little game was he playing now?

He smiled at her, infuriatingly. 'You've forgotten this.'

Camilla frowned. Her camera-bag. It had completely slipped her mind. Reluctantly, she released Eric's arm and began to walk back across the gravel towards Ross as, without conceding one single step, he stood there, holding out the bag. She stopped a couple of paces away. 'Thank you,' she said, still not looking at his face.

But then, as she reached out to take hold of the strap and swing it across her shoulder, suddenly he had moved towards her to provide an unwelcome helping hand. His hand brushed her arm and seemed to linger, making her flesh burn and her heart grow still. Involuntarily, her eyes shot up to meet his and she blanched inwardly at the ferocity of his gaze. Dark coals smouldered down at her, burning with an emotion she could not read. Yet his tone was composed and cool as he told her, 'So that's Eric. Just as I imagined him.' The dark eyes bored into her face. 'He looks like an exceedingly nice sort of bloke—but for someone else, not for you.'

'That's where you're wrong.' She glared at him. 'Eric is very much for me. So don't you try and interfere,' she warned. 'You'll be sorry if you do!'

Ross laughed at the pale threat and shook his head. 'Brave words,' he told her. 'But a little too late. I've already done all the interfering I need to do.

You may not fully realise it yet, but every time Eric kisses you from now on you'll remember what it was like to be kissed by me. Every time he lays a hand on you, your body will secretly ache for my touch.'

Such vanity! 'You think so, do you?'

'I know so.' His gaze brushed her face, then slid down burningly to caress her slim form. 'In spite of Eric's many certain attributes, marriage to a man like him will never fully satisfy the woman within you. Only one man in the world can do that, as you discovered for yourself yesterday afternoon.'

Camilla felt hot colour seep into her cheeks as his words transported her back to the little but'n'ben. 'But there's more to life than just sex!' she said tautly. It was no more than infernal arrogance on his part that he should, even for one single minute, expect her to give up everything for an occasional roll in the hay with him!

'*Just* sex? Is that all it was?'

She glanced away, her mask in fear of slipping. No one but herself would ever know, but it had been overwhelmingly, terrifyingly more than just sex. Amid those wild, unforgettable moments of passion, he had possessed more than her body. He had possessed her soul.

Smothering the suddenly bereft sensation that welled up treacherously inside her now, Camilla carefully composed her features and fixed him with a cold, stony look. 'Thank you for the bag. I'd better go now. Eric's waiting.'

'Yes, indeed.' His gaze was equally stony. 'You'd better not keep Eric waiting.'

For a moment their eyes held, like two mortal

enemies. Then, stiffly, without a backward glance, Camilla turned and walked back across the forecourt to Eric.

The next couple of days were tense and uneasy, though Eric's presence undoubtedly helped. He had decided to stay on in Glen Crannach until Camilla had finished shooting the collection. 'Then we can fly back to London together,' he had insisted. 'I was worried about you, you know, up here all on your own.'

Camilla had smiled bitterly to herself, knowing now that it would have been better if she had never come. All her worst premonitions had come true—and, though she would try her best to forget what had happened, she knew she would never be the same again. She would never be able to forget that day on Mhoire. Nor its bitter aftermath.

After they had made love that day, she and Ross had lain quietly in bed, arms wrapped loosely round each other. And even then Camilla had known that something inside her had changed. A bright, glowing feeling, secret and warm, the like of which she had never before known, suddenly seemed to illuminate her whole being.

And she knew what it was, there could be no doubt, though the realisation had come as a shock. Against all reason, against all sense, she had fallen desperately in love with him.

She had not at that moment dared to think of all the complications that must issue from this folly. For the moment it had simply been enough just to be lying in his arms.

It was Ross who had broken through her reverie.

Kissing her, he had turned on his side to look long and deeply into her eyes. 'You'll stay, of course? You won't go back to London now?'

Her heart had jolted in her breast. There was nothing in the world she wanted more. Yet caution had bade her ask with a smile, 'Tell me why I shouldn't go back.'

He had bent to plant a lingering kiss on her bare shoulder. 'Because I want you here with me. How can I make love to you if you're more than six hundred miles away?'

At his answer her heart had faltered a little. But she said nothing, just pressed her cheek against his.

'I want to make love to you, Camilla, day after day after day after day. And night after night after night after night.' He sighed a little and pulled her closer. 'You make me crazy for you. I could never get enough of you. I want you in my arms and in my bed. I want you with me at Castle Crannach.' He pulled back a little and searched her face. 'Isn't that, my love, what you want, too?'

She wanted it more than she could ever dare tell him. Almost more than she dared admit to herself. But one essential question still had to be answered. What, exactly, was he offering her?

She looked back into his eyes, her heart beating wildly. 'I want you, too.' She flushed a little. 'But, Ross, I——'

'No buts.' He kissed her face, one hand moving softly to cup her breast. 'Do you remember what I told you?' he went on to ask.

'Told me? When?' she wanted to know.

'On the ferry to Mhoire.' He held her eyes. 'Surely you can't have forgotten that?'

Of course she hadn't. She shook her head. He had told her of the one special love he was seeking and of how he would settle for nothing less. 'I remember,' she assured him a little stiffly—for, surely, he could not be referring to that? Though she'd have given her life for it to be otherwise, cupid's dart, she felt certain, had pierced only one heart.

Which meant he must be referring to that other subject—his affairs, or 'occasional diversions', as he'd called them, and his observation that she should follow in his footsteps.

The deduction chilled her. She could not meet his eyes, as he invited once more, 'So, will you stay, Camilla?'

She took a deep breath. 'Let me get this straight. You want me to move into Castle Crannach?'

As he nodded, she held her breath and waited. Just one word of commitment. That was all she asked. But when he spoke at last it was only to tell her, 'I shall make love to you, my darling, morning, noon and night.'

'You must be out of your damned head!' Her tone was harsh as she pushed him away, harsh with the pain and disappointment that tore through her. 'What makes you think I'd want to come and stay with you? I don't want your lovemaking, Ross McKeown! I thought I'd already made it quite clear? I'm virtually engaged to Eric!'

Her legs had been trembling as she'd staggered from the bed, her brain exploding like fireworks inside her head. To think she'd been on the brink of turning her back on the man who loved her and wanted to marry her!

For she had been poised to do just that. In one rash, reckless moment she would have given up everything—and for a man who dared to offer her in exchange no more than a cheap and tawdry affair!

He had pushed his case no further then. With a look like thunder on his face, he had risen from the bed and towered over her, magnificent in his naked manliness. 'At last I understand,' he had ground contemptuously. 'A one-night stand was all you were after. Forgive me for being a little slow. I guess I'm just not used to your big-city ways.'

'I guess you're not!' she had blazed back furiously, hiding the wounds his words had inflicted. One thing was for certain, he would never know now what her true feelings for him were. These she would keep locked away inside her, and pray that they would die one day.

In the meantime, she had not set eyes on Ross since that last bitter exchange outside the castle, and she had spoken to him, briefly, only once. He had phoned her at the hotel to let her know that the disappearance of the jewels had been solved.

'As I suspected, Maggie took them. It appears that, like you, she believes in the curse. She got her son to take them over to Mhoire and hide them in the keep. He was the young man Davie told us about. Both of them have made a full confession.'

So it had been Maggie, the last person she had suspected. In spite of herself, Camilla suddenly felt a dart of sympathy for the dour-faced woman. 'Are you going to prosecute?' she asked.

There was a short pause before he answered. 'Not in the circumstances, no. Their motives, as they say, were at least honourable. Though they'll both be in very deep trouble indeed if they should ever attempt such a thing again.'

He paused once more. 'That's it, then,' he told her. 'Unless, of course, you have anything to tell me?'

She could tell by the change in his tone of voice exactly to what he was referring. 'I have nothing to tell you,' she answered flatly. Did he really expect that she might have reconsidered his insulting offer to become his mistress? The notion was both hurtful and offensive.

'I see,' he had answered, and hung up the phone.

Over the next couple of days, on her trips to the collection room, as she gradually wound up her assignment, the old Laird accompanied her with the key. Quite obviously Ross was avoiding her, which was probably the most chivalrous thing he could do. Yet, all the same, she did not feel free of him. She could feel his presence, like a heavy dark shadow, seeming to monitor every breath she took.

By day, when she was with Eric, she could occasionally block out the sensation, but at night, as she lay alone in her bed, he seemed to take her over body and soul. And as she wept endless, bitter tears into her pillow, through her pain she felt a terrible guilt. What had passed between herself and Ross must remain a secret forever from Eric, and she deeply regretted the deceit that entailed. But she would make it up to Eric. Though he would never move her as she had been moved by this wild Highlander she would devote her life to making him happy.

That would be her life's mission.

And her penance.

'So, that's settled, then? We go to the old Laird's birthday party and leave for London the following day. I'll phone the airport and book our flights as soon as we get back to the hotel.'

They were driving back from a trip to the coast, Eric at the wheel. With a pang, Camilla glanced across at him. Was their departure really so imminent? Though she knew she should be glad, in her heart she was not. With an effort, she focused on what Eric had been saying. 'I really think we ought to go to the party,' she answered. 'I like the old Laird. I wouldn't want to be rude.'

'Of course.' Eric nodded and reached across to touch her hand. 'He seems a nice enough old gentleman. A bit eccentric, of course. But if that's what you want, then we shall go.'

Camilla smiled as she glanced across at him. In Eric's book anyone who failed to comply rigidly to City standards was considered a little bit eccentric. She squeezed his hand fondly before he snatched it away to negotiate a particularly tricky bend, swearing politely to himself as he did so. These 'damned medieval country roads, fit for nothing but a donkey cart', as he so scathingly described them over the past couple of days had stretched his temper.

'The sooner we get back to Oxford Street and Piccadilly, the happier I'll be,' he professed. 'These wretched little dirt tracks are far too full of surprises for me.'

Never was spoken a truer word. Right on cue, as they rounded the bend, they found their path blocked solid by a flock of sheep!

Eric brought the car to a juddering halt and let out a decidedly colourful oath. And, somehow, in that instant, Camilla knew precisely what he was about to do next. Quick as a flash she reached across and laid her hand across the horn, just a fortunate fraction of a second before Eric's fist came down on it.

'Don't !' she admonished hastily. 'Don't bang the horn. You'll only frighten them.'

'Then how the devil am I supposed to persuade them to get out of our way?'

'There'll be someone with them.' She craned her neck. 'There's bound to be. They won't be alone.' She glanced round at either side of the road, suddenly half expecting the figure of Ross McKeown to come bursting through the trees.

At the image a sudden sharp longing pierced through her and hot, foolish tears sprang to her eyes. Impatiently, she blinked them away. If she was to forget him, she must try harder.

'Here I am! Just give me a minute and I'll soon have these beasts out of your way!' A ruddy-cheeked man in dungarees and carrying a shepherd's crook had suddenly appeared from nowhere, a black and white collie dog at his heels. He grinned good-naturedly at the occupants of the car, then he whistled and the dog went into action.

The very instant the road was cleared, Eric slammed the engine into first and drove past, much too fast. 'Damned sheep shouldn't be allowed on the road. If you ask me, it's a damned disgrace.'

Instantly, Camilla sprang to the shepherd's defence. 'But this isn't Knightsbridge, you know.

Here different rules apply. In this part of the world, animals of the four-legged variety have as much right to use the highways as two-legged animals and their cars——'

She stopped abruptly, realising what she was saying—almost exactly word for word what Ross had told her that first time they'd met. A fearsome flood of anguish gushed inside her. She swallowed on the sudden hard lump in her throat. Was it really possible that even that, their very first conversation—their very first quarrel, more correctly!—was stamped so indelibly on her memory? Would she never be free of the man?

On an impulse, she leaned closer to Eric and lovingly put her hand on his knee. She reached up and kissed him on the temple.

'Don't worry,' she told him, squeezing his knee. 'Only two more days to go—and then we'll be back in London, with no more silly sheep to bother us.'

And no more Ross McKeown to haunt me, she added fervently to herself.

But though she knew in her head that was as she wanted it—Ross finally, irrevocably, a relic of the past—she had to hold very tightly to Eric's leg to block out the sudden hollow feeling that crept, like a chill wind, into her heart.

It promised to be a difficult evening. Camilla glanced nervously at her reflection in the mirror. She was not looking forward to it at all.

For the Laird's seventy-eighth birthday party she had picked out the only dressy outfit that she had brought along with her—a dark blue Nicole Farhi dress whose clever cut was both simple and elegant—and had stylishly caught back her glossy blonde hair in a pair of pretty gilt combs. In her ears she wore a pair of gold drop earrings and a matching circle of gold around her neck.

'You look terrific,' Eric told her when she joined him downstairs in the lobby. He kissed her cheek and took her arm. 'Come on. Let's go. I'll drive tonight.'

They arrived at Castle Crannach, as requested, a little after eight o'clock. Maggie looking not the least bit repentant and just as taciturn as ever, showed them through to the drawing-room where the Laird and his small group of guests were assembled.

Camilla stepped into the elegant room, one arm clutched tightly around Eric's, a plastic party smile pinned to her face. And the very first person her eyes fell upon was the distinguished dark figure by the tall casement windows who had turned momentarily to observe her entrance. And in spite of her resolve to treat him with indifference, her jaw dropped and her heart lurched wildly inside her breast. Never in her life before had she seen a man look quite so splendid.

She was used to seeing Eric in a suit. He very rarely wore anything else. But this was the very first time she had seen Ross dressed in anything other than jeans. The transformation took her breath away.

The plain dark navy suit he wore, with its razor-sharp tailoring and made-to-measure fit, seemed superficially to tame the raw, dark animal power of him. The sometimes wild dark hair was swept back cleanly from his face, and his handsome tanned features seemed chiselled more finely above the gleaming whiteness of his shirt. Yet the innate authority he exuded was quite undiminished by his civilised attire. As always, he dominated the room quite effortlessly.

With a fierce and sorrowful squeeze of the heart, Camilla dropped her eyes away. Here was a side to him she had never before seen, yet as natural and true as all the others had been. For, quite clearly, he was a man who could mix with beggars and kings, and command deference and respect from any of them.

Detaching himself from the group by the window, Ross came towards them on unhurried strides. 'Welcome,' he told them, his tone polite, but notably lacking in any degree of warmth. The iron-grey eyes rested for a moment on her face. 'All set for the journey back south tomorrow? I imagine you can't wait to get on that plane.'

It was true, yet desperately untrue, and as Camilla endeavoured to look steadily back at him she wondered if her torn emotions showed. 'There's nothing to keep me here any more,' she informed him in an even tone. 'My job is done. It's time to move on.'

'Quite so.' He smiled a cutting smile. 'We all of us have to get on with our lives.' For a moment the dark eyes bored right through her. Then, with an elegantly dismissive gesture, he deliberately turned his attention to Eric. 'Come and pay your respects to my grandfather. He's the reason we're all here, after all.'

At least Angus McKeown seemed pleased to see them. Looking distinguished and jaunty in kilt and hose, he beamed delightedly at Camilla as she and

Eric approached his little group. 'I'm so glad you could make it, lass. Let me introduce you to some of my friends.'

In other circumstances the evening would have been enjoyable. The Laird's guests, mostly friends and neighbours from round about, were a boisterous, good-humoured lot and the conversation was entertaining and lively, with only one faintly jarring note, just as coffee was being served.

A red-haired man in Highland rig suddenly leaned across the table to Ross. 'So, how about the big race tomorrow? Are you all set?' he wanted to know.

As Ross smiled modestly, Camilla's heart lurched. Big race, the man had said. Surely that could only mean one thing?

Another of the guests instantly confirmed her fears. 'Oh, don't worry,' he was saying brightly. 'By this time tomorrow, Ross, without a doubt, is going to be the new five hundred cc champion.'

As a murmur of agreement went round the table, Ross sat back and smiled unaffectedly. 'If I am, I'll treat you all to a drink in the Stag tomorrow night,' he promised. Then he glanced across, deliberately, at Camilla. 'What a pity you won't be here to join in the celebrations, if there are any.'

She returned his glance, suppressing all emotion. 'Yes, what a pity,' she agreed. 'I'll try to think of you when I'm down in London.'

On the excuse that they had an early plane to catch, Camilla and Eric left soon after that. She kept the goodbyes deliberately brief, though she warmly squeezed the old Laird's hand as she kissed him farewell. In the brief course of their acquaintance she had grown genuinely fond of the old man, and she felt foolish tears rise to her eyes as he confirmed that the feeling was mutual.

'I'm going to miss you, you know,' he told her. 'If you're ever up in these parts again, be sure to drop in and see us.'

'I will,' she promised falsely, knowing in her heart that she would never dare to pass this way again—a decision which Ross's curt farewell handshake told her he more than fully endorsed.

They stepped out into the pale light of a crescent moon—and were half way across the forecourt to the car when, to her annoyance, Camilla realised that she had left her bag behind. Damn! She hesitated, half tempted just to go on without it, then make a phone call from the hotel. That way she would not risk encountering Ross. He would more than likely entrust one of his lackeys with the task of delivering it to the hotel.

But Eric was all for going back. 'Come on, I'll come with you. It won't take a minute,' he urged.

Camilla shook her head. 'No, I'll go alone. It'll be less of a fuss that way.' Alone, she could perhaps slip back into the castle without drawing attention to herself, retrieve the bag from where she knew she'd left it, then slip out again unnoticed.

With a good-natured shrug, Eric agreed. 'OK. I'll wait here.'

She walked quickly across the gravel, heels crunching, then up the stone steps. For some reason she felt nervous, her breathing quick and shallow in her breast. The bag, she knew, was in the dining-room, propped against the legs of her chair.

The guests had adjourned some time ago for more coffee and brandy, to the drawing-room next door. She hurried on tiptoe across the hall. It appeared the coast was clear.

But the bag was not where she had left it. She circled the table impatiently, searching, eyes pinned to the floor. Where could it have gone? Who could have taken it? Could she have been mistaken, after all?

'Is this what you're looking for, perhaps?'

She whirled round, startled, at the sound of a deep voice, to see Ross standing watching her from the open doorway. In one hand he held her bag. He raised it up and cocked one eyebrow. 'Maggie found it,' he informed her coolly. 'I was pretty sure it belonged to you.' The dark eyes regarded her face for a moment. 'A neat trick.' He smiled at her. 'At last, our chance to be alone.'

Camilla blinked, only half comprehending. The unexpected sight him of had fuddled her brain. 'Trick?' she repeated. 'What are you talking about? I simply came back here to get my bag.'

'Such innocence.' He smiled at her, as he stepped through the doorway into the room. 'If I weren't better acquainted with the woman underneath I might actually believe in the childlike innocence shining from those wide blue eyes.' With a far from innocent look in his own eyes he closed the door behind him with a provocative click.

Every muscle in Camilla's body suddenly seemed to stiffen in defence. He had been waiting for her, and she had walked straight into his trap. 'Give me my bag,' she demanded curtly. 'You know very well I didn't plan anything. You may enjoy playing devious little games, but right now I'm afraid I'm not in the mood for them.'

'No?' With a harsh, wicked smile, he came towards her. 'So what are you in the mood for, Camilla?' He laid the bag on the table and stood purposefully over her. 'Don't be shy. What's on your mind?'

She could have snatched the bag and run, then escaped out into the corridor before he could stop her. But something held her—some light in his eyes, or possibly just the sudden frantic beating of her heart. She stood mutely staring at him as he continued, 'I rather thought we might take this opportunity for a final little chat.'

'What sort of chat?' She regarded him suspiciously. 'You and I have already said to one another everything we could possibly have to say.'

'You think so?' With a light smile, he lowered himself to the table edge, the somehow relaxed and easy gesture minutely reducing the tension between them. His eyes were level with her own as he told her, 'There are a lot of things I haven't said yet. Like how particularly stunning you're looking tonight.'

Camilla felt an awkward smile flutter across her lips. Foolishly, the compliment had pleased her, and she felt half tempted to return it. He too was looking particularly stunning tonight after all. More stunning than a man had any right to look. But she stopped herself. He had no need of her kind words. 'Don't tell me you went to all the trouble of trapping me in here just to tell me that,' she said scathingly instead.

'Not exactly.' He held her eyes, making her stomach curl up inside. 'I was just wondering if you'd done any more thinking about my invitation to stay here with me.'

If she had not known him better, just for a moment she might have thought she caught a note of entreaty in his voice. But that was mere whimsy on her part, she decided swiftly, answering, as she did so, 'I could think about it from here to eternity and my answer would never be any different.' Amorous diversions just for the hell of it might appeal to him, but they weren't for her. She felt herself stiffen with indignation. And he had a monstrous nerve proposing such a thing!

But the man was without shame. He continued, without blinking, 'You're making a big mistake, you know.'

She glared at him with glittering blue eyes. 'You're the one who's making a mistake!'

'You think so?' He spoke the words as a challenge, his tall frame straightening as he rose from the table. 'Perhaps, Camilla, you have already forgotten . . .?'

'Forgotten?' Instinctively, she took a step back.

'Yes, forgotten, Camilla.' With a movement, he closed the gap between them. 'Perhaps you need a small reminder.'

She wanted to flee. She wanted to stay. For she knew exactly what was going to happen next. Like a helpless stray deer startled by headlights, she stood transfixed by the burning dark eyes, fearing what he was about to do, yet with her whole body suddenly longing for it.

As his hand reached out, she closed her eyes, her heart pounding as his fingers touched her hair. Then she shivered and let her body slacken against him as his free hand softly circled her waist and, in one soft yet impatient movement, Ross drew her close to him. Suddenly, she was pressed against him. She could feel his heat, his hardness, his strength, the delicious, overpowering urgency in him as her breasts were crushed against the wall of his chest.

Then the breath left her body and the universe stood still as, hungrily, his lips pressed down on hers.

Pain pierced through her, or was it pleasure? She could no longer tell. And for one brief, wild and heady moment she no longer cared. Greedy for his touch, she clung to him, her arms circling his neck, caressing his hair, her senses on fire from his plundering kisses and the swift, excited race of his heart against hers.

'Camilla, Camilla.' The words were a groan as one hand slipped round to cover her breast, and even before his thumb found her nipple she felt it lengthen excitedly and grow hard. Desire went lancing through her loins as he thrust his hips against her now, leaving her in no doubt at all about the fullness of his own arousal.

Deep in her throat she moaned as a fire of passion swept through her veins. Perhaps one last time would do no harm, she was telling herself through the fog in her brain. One last wild and wanton time, right here on the dining-room floor.

But it was at that moment that he broke the spell. He drew away from her just a fraction and looked burningly down into her eyes. 'Forget about Eric,' he demanded hoarsely. 'Don't go back to London. Stay here with me.'

It was enough to bring her back to her senses. Horrified, she drew away. 'No! Never!' she cried.

'Never! Don't ask me to!' Then with sudden strength and determination she tore herself roughly from his grasp. 'Eric's the man I'm going to marry! I've told you that right from the start!'

'And I've tried to tell you from the start that he's not the man for you!'

At the fierce look in his eyes, sudden panic overtook her. If she was foolish enough to stay one moment more, there was a danger he might turn her life upside-down. In a heartbeat, panic turned to terror. She knew only one thing. She must escape.

Blindly, before he could stop her, she grabbed her bag and raced for the door. And she dared not stop running until she had reached the safety of Eric, and the car.

CHAPTER NINE

THE plane rose up above the early-morning mists, circled briefly, then headed south. In approximately one hour's time it was due to land in London.

From her window seat Camilla gazed down, sudden emptiness flooding her heart. So, it was goodbye forever, after all. She should be feeling relieved, but she did not.

Last night she had scarcely slept at all. Thoughts of Ross had crowded her brain, scaring off sleep, cruelly tormenting her. Even when at last she had finally drifted off, he had refused to let her be, coming to her in her dreams, filling her unconsciousness.

She had dreamed that she was pregnant, and happy to be so, with Ross's child. And so sharp and vivid had been the dream that she had awakened with a start, for the very first time since that afternoon on Mhoire facing this very real possibility. Until that moment it had never crossed her mind that those hours of love making in the little but'n'ben could have resulted in the creation of a child. In her mind they had been hours suspended, fantasy hours, detached from reality, the whole thing a passing, barely real event that had no power to touch her everyday life.

Oddly, the realisation that this was not so had soothed her as much as it alarmed her. Emotionally exhausted, she had closed her eyes then and had slept dreamlessly till dawn.

This morning, however, she had awakened to discover that all was normal. She was not with child. Wryly she had checked the dates in her diary. She was two days early. In the cold, clear, rational light of day, she had suddenly felt immensely relieved.

For some strange, illogical reason, however, her mood had changed as they had left the hotel. All the way to Inverness, feigning tiredness as her excuse, she had barely spoken a word. By the time they had arrived at the airport she had felt herself grow even more withdrawn. Then, as the plane had taken off, an icy numbness had settled in her soul. She had known then, without a doubt, that she was leaving something immeasurably precious behind.

Feeling Eric's eyes on her, she gave herself a mental shake and turned towards him with a smile.

'Are you all right.' His face wore a frown. The light blue eyes were full of concern.

Camilla kept her smile pinned tight and rested one hand on his sleeve. 'Sure I'm all right,' she assured him breezily. 'Just a little tired, that's all.'

The frown never lifted. 'You've been so quiet. I've never known you to be like this before.'

With a stab of guilt she patted his arm. 'It's nothing. Believe me. I'm just tired.'

Eric nodded. 'If you say so.' He seemed to consider in silence for a moment. Then the blue eyes narrowed as he turned towards her. 'But it's not just today I've noticed it, Camilla. You've been acting strangely since I arrived.'

'Strangely?' She felt a warm flush touch her

cheeks as she forced a dismissive little laugh. 'That's a funny thing to say. What on earth do you mean by that?'

'I don't know exactly.' Eric paused. He seemed to think deeply for a moment, carefully selecting his words. Then his hand closed lightly over hers as he continued, his voice strangely detached, 'I somehow couldn't help suspecting that something was going on between you and Ross.'

Almost simultaneously, the colour ebbed then rose again in Camilla's guilty face. She swallowed, feeling her mouth go dry. 'But, Eric,' she protested, 'that's preposterous!'

His gaze didn't flicker. He held her eyes. 'Is it?' he wanted to know.

'But of course it is! Ross and me? Why, we can barely stand the sight of one another!'

Thoughtfully, Eric pursed his lips. He sighed and glanced down at his shoes. 'That was what I thought at first, and then I wasn't sure. I could sense there was an antagonism between you, but it wasn't the antagonism of hate. It seemed to me more like the antagonism between two people who are fighting something within themselves. Two incredibly like-minded people unable to get to grips with their feelings.'

He paused and glanced across at Camilla, who had frozen in her seat. In a bleak and faintly horrified way, she felt mesmerised by what he was saying.

With another small sigh he carried on. 'I came rushing up here because I was worried about you. When I got that garbled message about you having gone off to the Hebrides, I felt I had to come up and find out what was going on. Then, as soon as I saw you with Ross, I had a nasty feeling that I knew.' He paused and smiled a doleful smile. 'Did you notice that over the past few days I never once brought up the subject of my proposal? The omission was deliberate. I was rather hoping you might.'

Hot colour rushed to Camilla's face. Suddenly, she could not meet his gaze. For all her insistence to Ross that Eric was the man she was going to marry, it was days since she had thought seriously about his marriage proposal. Since his arrival, it had rarely crossed her mind. She opened her mouth to offer an apology, perhaps even a rickety explanation, but, before she could speak, Eric cut in, his tone even and faintly self-deprecating.

'You know, I'm not the tunnel-visioned City professional that some people take me for. I see things—and I understand you perhaps a great deal better than you think I do. I know very well the reasons why you would have married me. What I have to offer you is what one part of you very badly needs. Security, stability, a family of your own. But I also happen to know, Camilla, that there's a great deal more to you than that.'

He held up his hand to silence her as she started to protest. 'You have a wild, artistic side, a need for freedom, adventure, romance. And, deep in my heart, I've always feared that that was a side of you I could never satisfy. Which was why I deliberately gave you time to think about my proposal before you gave me your answer. I thought a week alone up in the Highlands would give you the time and space you needed.' He grimaced wryly and shook his head. 'Needless to say, I hadn't reckoned on Ross McKeown coming on the scene.'

His words had shocked her into silence—for each syllable of them was true. Though she cared for Eric, perhaps she had always known, somewhere deep down in her soul, that she wanted more from life than he could give her. She had tried to smother her doubts—and might well have succeeded, if only Ross had not come along. The sudden realisation shamed her. She glanced away guiltily.

Kindly, without rancour, he took her hand. 'The only reason I say all this is because I love you, Camilla. But I fear I could never make you happy, and that would make me unhappy too.' He took a deep breath. 'Though I hope that we can always remain friends, I'm not the man that you should marry. I think, if we're honest, we both know that the man for you is Ross McKeown.'

Camilla's heart turned over in her breast. 'Ross McKeown?' she whispered painfully. Just the sound of his name made her weak inside.

Eric smiled and kissed her cheek. 'Well—you're in love with him, aren't you?'

She stared at him foolishly. Oh, yes! she longed to answer. Hopelessly, helplessly, utterly, shamelessly! But he doesn't love me, she mumbled inwardly. All he wants of me is my body.

'Whatever differences exist between you, I feel sure that they can be sorted out.' Eric was glancing at his watch as he spoke. 'We're due to land in about ten minutes' time. If you want my advice, you'll catch the first plane back to Inverness.'

She was on it, heading northwards through a clear

blue sky, just over an hour later.

In spite of her nervousness, her heart bubbled over. It was possible that he would not want to see her, that this whole crazy mission was a foolish mistake. But, right or wrong, she had to make this journey, and if his offer was still open she intended to accept it.

The hour-long journey seemed to take forever, but at last they were touching down again. She stared eagerly out at the mountainous landscape, once so strange and threatening, now so close to her heart, then impatiently made her way down the aisle, then down the gangway on to the tarmac. Already she could smell him in the clear, clean air. Her heart gave a jubilant little lift.

The hire car she had booked from London was ready and waiting for her at the airport. Without even so much as a glance at her map, she threw her few things into the back and headed straight for Castle Crannach. This time, she sensed, there would be no wrong turnings. Her heart and her instincts would show her the way.

It was just after eleven o'clock when she drew up in the castle forecourt, pleased and relieved to observe the dusty Land Rover parked to one side. On legs that seemed to float above the ground, she strode up the stone steps to the front door, knocked twice and waited, her pulses racing.

The door opened and Maggie was standing there—and for the very first time in Camilla's presence the stern face broke into a smile. 'Miss Holden, what a surprise! I thought you'd gone back to London.'

'I had.' Camilla made a face. 'But I've come back

again.' As Maggie stepped aside, Camilla walked into the hall. 'I've come to see the Honourable Ross McKeown.'

Maggie glanced up at her and frowned. 'I'm afraid Mr Ross isn't here. He's gone off on that noisy great machine of his to some motorbike race at Crannach Head.'

Camilla faltered. In all the turmoil of the past twelve hours, she had completely forgotten about the race. But, as she hesitated, momentarily thrown, wondering what to do next, a stooped and grey-haired figure appeared at the far end of the hall. He was smiling broadly, like a schoolboy, as he came towards her.

'Down the road, about five miles, turn left at the church, then follow the road.' Angus McKeown rattled off the directions with a knowing twinkle in his eyes. He seemed pleased and not at all surprised to see her standing once more in his hall. 'You can't miss it,' he urged her. 'Off you go. Be the first to congratulate the new local champion.'

Camilla needed no second bidding. Already she was racing back down the steps, diving behind the wheel of her car and screeching off in the direction the old Laird had said. But now a new emotion tugged at her heart, along with the eagerness she felt. A knife-like twist of apprehension for the danger she sensed Ross might be in.

Angus had been right. She could not miss it. Already, a couple of miles away from the track where the races were being held, she could smell the petrol fumes and the stench of scorched rubber, and hear the roar and whine of the huge machines. Heart thudding anxiously, she parked her car in the car park and hurried through the milling crowd, forcing her way towards the front, neck craning impatiently for a glimpse of Ross.

A score of helmeted, leather-clad riders were lining up along the track with their bikes for the start of a new race, but Camilla's eyes homed in instantly on the tall figure in black at the end of the line. The arrogant broad shoulders and the powerful thighs that hugged the dark metal of his machine could belong to no other man but Ross.

Unaware of her presence, he half turned towards her, so that she caught a fleeting glimpse of the forceful, rugged lines of his face before he snapped down the visor of his helmet, pulled on his gauntlets and kicked his machine into life. But in that tiny fraction of a second Camilla knew that she had been right to come.

Suddenly, through her fear, her heart was dancing, overcome by the warm and fierce emotion that seemed to fill her very soul. 'I love you,' she murmured, 'and I'll love you on your terms—for never in my life will I love like this again.'

But before she could present him with her change of heart, there was the ordeal of the race to get through. With a flash of black fear she thought of the curse and felt a shiver down her spine. 'If anything should happen to him now,' she murmured, 'I know that I would never survive.'

As the flag came down and the riders roared off, she could scarcely bear to keep her eyes on them. At every bend and on every corner she seemed to die a thousand deaths. With every acceleration, her heart stood still and a silent prayer escaped her lips. Anxious perspiration beaded her brow and glistened on her upper lip, and her fists were clenched so ferociously tight that the nails dug like talons into her flesh.

And there was one terrible moment. One rider who had been tailing Ross, who for the past two laps had been in the lead, suddenly made an all-out effort to overtake him on the inside bend. But the move was badly calculated. The rider momentarily lost control of his bike—and for one hideous, nauseating second it seemed the two bikes might collide. By the time Camilla dared breathe again, Ross had extricated himself from the danger with one almighty acceleration.

Still half stunned by that moment of fear and her overwhelming sense of relief, she almost failed to register the lowering of the chequered flag. Then a mighty roar went up from the crowd and pride jostled with love and relief in her heart. Without thinking, Camilla began to barge her way through the crowd, tears in her eyes, towards the champion.

He saw her just a fraction of a second before she threw herself into his arms. In one movement the helmet was tossed aside and his arms were about her, pulling her close. And he only had time to murmur throatily before his lips swooped down on hers, 'You've come back! Oh, thank heavens! This time I'll never let you leave.'

Wide-eyed with wonder and delight, Camilla gazed down at the bundle in her arms. Could this tiny, exquisite creature with his unruly tufts of silky black hair really belong to herself and Ross? Was it possible that their love had made him? Could they truly have been so blessed?

Her heart aching with happiness, she glanced round at the flower-festooned drawing-room in which she sat, then let her eyes slide lovingly to the dark-haired man at her side. She held the baby up to him. 'Do you want to hold him?' she smiled.

Gently, proudly, Ross lifted his son and held him softly against his broad chest, his movements confident and unselfconscious, as though he'd been handling babies all his life. Camilla watched him and smiled, feeling the quickening of love deep in her heart. It seemed impossible now to believe that she could ever have doubted her future lay with him.

A lot had happened since that day at the racetrack, just over a year ago, though, like the day of their wedding and the birth of their son, it was a day that she would never forget.

She remembered how he had dragged her away as soon as the presentation of the cups was over, his dark eyes burning and intense as he'd demanded to know the reason for her return.

'You,' she had told him simply. 'I'm not going to marry Eric, after all.'

The relief had been vivid in his face, though he had at once demanded a fuller explanation. 'How come?' he had wanted to know. 'What happened between here and London?'

She had looked into his eyes, loving him, adoring him, and knowing that the feeling would last forever. He might only consent to give her a little of his time—maybe only a few months, maybe a year—but to have him, even for so short a time, would be worth any sacrifice in the world.

'I had a little chat with Eric,' she confessed. 'Or

rather, he had a little chat with me. He convinced me that we were wrong for each other, that it would be a big mistake for us to marry.'

To her mild surprise, Ross didn't crow. He didn't even say, I told you so. Instead, he murmured softly, 'Good for Eric. I had him figured for a man with some sense.'

Camilla couldn't resist giving his ribs a little poke. 'After all the cruel things you've said about Eric! You've never had a single good word to say for him!'

His eyes remained sober as he caught her in his arms and looked down intently into her face. 'The things I said about Eric, my love, were never intended to diminish him. I have enormous respect for men like Eric. They're decent, honest and upright men.' The wide mouth pursed, as his grip on her tightened. 'But that didn't stop me from knowing from the start that the man he is is not the man for you.' As he kissed her nose, his expression lightened. 'What you need is a wild reprobate like me.'

Camilla laughed and leaned against him. Never had he spoken a truer word!

'If I seemed to come down a bit hard on Eric at times,' Ross assured her, nuzzling her hair, 'it was simply because I had to find a way to convince you that marriage to him would be a terrible mistake.' He kissed her temple, making her shiver. 'Drastic situations call for drastic measures.'

Then, with firm, gentle fingers, he eased her away from him to look down directly into her eyes. 'But that's only half the answer you've given me so far. You've told me why you've finished with Eric, but you've still to explain why you came to me.'

How could she explain it? Sudden shyness surged through her, making her cheeks glow pinkly and her eyes falter from his.

She could feel him standing over her, waiting for her answer, one inquisitive dark eyebrow raised—and she could not say 'love', dared not speak of such emotions, could not bring herself to open up her heart to him. For the first time since she had boarded the plane in London, she felt a tiny dart of pain. The reason she could not reveal the love that burned within her was because no answering flame of love burned within him.

Silently she chastised herself. She had known that, and accepted it, before she came. Resolutely, she looked up at him and gave him her answer.

'I came,' she said, 'because some force inside me—a force I cannot and no longer wish to resist—has been drawing me to you since first we met.'

There! It was not a lie, just a slight diminution of the truth.

Ross kissed her. 'Oh, Camilla. Then you feel it, too?' But as he held her close she asked a question of her own—though she knew, all too well, in advance, the answer.

'And you? Why did you ask me to stay?'

There was a pause that made her heart stand still as he brushed back her hair and looked hard into her eyes, and for a moment she was tempted to withdraw the question, wondering if she could bear to the hear the truth out loud. Would it not be wiser, her anguished heart was crying, to shut out the truth and just pretend? But it was too late for that. Already he was saying, 'Remember what I told you about my being an impossible romantic that day on the ferry to Mhoire?'

She nodded bleakly. 'I remember.' And she steeled herself to hear what she must hear.

His hand had remained tangled in her hair, his fingers pressing warmly against her scalp. And he was forcing her to look at him, as though to ensure there could be no misunderstandings with what he was about to say.

'I told you I believed in a very special love and that I would settle for nothing less.'

Camilla nodded. 'Yes, I remember that.'

'I also told you——' He paused.

Camilla swallowed. This was the bit she dreaded to hear.

'I also told you——' He paused again, the dark eyes unrelentingly fixed on her face. 'I told you I would know who the girl for me was just by looking into her eyes.'

Camilla frowned. This was not what she had been expecting.

'Well——' He took a deep breath. 'I omitted to tell you I already knew who she was—and that I happened to be looking straight at her at the time.'

As his eyes smiled a softly quizzical smile, Camilla stared back at him in mute astonishment. He was talking in riddles. What did this mean?

'What I'm trying to tell you, Camilla darling, is that I'd already decided you were the girl for me. I suspected it the first moment I saw you, and I knew it for sure that night with the deer. Seeing you crouched by its side in tears, I finally saw behind that brave, brittle mask of yours. That was when I knew I loved you. That was when I decided you had to be my wife.'

It was too much for Camilla to take in. Her brain was reeling as she heard herself protest, 'But I thought all you wanted was an affair!'

'An affair!' Almost ferociously, he gripped her arm. 'Is that what *you* want? An affair!'

'No, of course not.' Startled, she blinked up at him. 'That was why I went away. But I couldn't stay away.' She bit her lip. 'So I came back to——' She broke off, embarrassed, suddenly unable to carry on.

'Camilla, Camilla, what have I done to you? How could I have made you believe such a thing?' Real anguish settled on his handsome face as he pulled her roughly into his arms. 'When I told you on Mhoire that I wanted to make love to you morning, noon and night, I did not for one moment mean for you to be my mistress. What I wanted then and what I want now is to make love to you forever as my wife!'

As she sighed, all the hurt and fear leaving her body, he pulled her even closer still. 'Forgive me, Camilla, for explaining myself so badly. It's just that I felt so close to you that day that I foolishly felt explanations weren't really necessary. I felt we understood each other without the need for words.'

She had felt that, too, but her old insecurities had intruded, clouding and marring the magic between them. She looked up at him now and told him truly, 'I had never felt so close to anyone in my life.'

He kissed her face. 'My love, my love. Let there never be another misunderstanding between us all our lives.' As she kissed him back a smile crept into his eyes. 'And there was me thinking that our trip to Mhoire, after all, had been a waste of time.'

Camilla frowned, uncomprehending. 'But we found the jewels. That's what we went for.'

'It's not what I went for, my sweet. I didn't think for one moment that we'd find the jewels there—though, happily, I was proved wrong. I took you to the island because I was hoping that, if I could get you to myself for a while, I might manage to persuade you not to marry Eric.'

'You devious creature!' She prodded him playfully—though inwardly she blessed his deviousness. For it was undoubtedly during those two days on Mhoire that her love for him had crystallised.

But his eyes had grown serious again. He gave her a gentle little shake. 'It may have slipped your mind, young lady, but I haven't had my answer yet. I have just made a very unambiguous proposal of marriage—and, unlike your previous patient suitors, I demand an answer right away!'

She'd looked up at him then, her eyes and mind clear, without a fraction of doubt or hesitation in her mind. 'I'll be your wife,' she had told him simply. 'I'll love you and cherish you for all of my life.'

'And I you for all of mine.' Fiercely, he'd looked down into her eyes. 'I'll make you happy, Camilla,' he had promised. 'Never doubt it. I know I can.'

She knew it, too. And over the past twelve months he had proved it true in at least a thousand ways. Camilla had never before suspected that there were so many different ways of being happy.

There had been the sheer, extravagant happiness of their wedding day on Ross's thirty-fifth birthday, the happiness of discovering she was pregnant, the simple day-to-day happiness of just being together. And the thrill of deep and sensuous happiness she felt each time he reached for her in the night. In the sometimes languorous, sometimes frenzied joining of their bodies all the love and joy of their union seemed magically expressed.

And she had a lifetime of such happiness to look forward to, she thought with an immense sense of wonder. It was all so much more than she had ever dared to dream.

The door of the drawing-room where they sat now opened and Maggie came in. Smiling, she crossed the room and gently took the baby from Ross. 'I'll take him off your hands for a while. Give you both a bit of a rest.'

Camilla smiled. 'You can bathe him, if you like. I'll be up to feed him in half an hour.' Then she watched as, beaming, Maggie left the room. Already, the good woman was as fiercely protective of the tiny week-old infant as she had once been of Ross.

Ross slipped an arm round Camilla's shoulder as she glanced up at the cards on the mantelpiece. Cards of congratulation from friends and relatives—including one from Anni and Sue of Focus, with whom, though she had relinquished her share of the company, she still kept in touch, and one particularly cherished one from Eric and his new wife.

She leaned her cheek against Ross's chin and glanced up into the dark grey eyes. She had a great deal to be grateful to Eric for, and she was glad that he and Ross had become friends.

He kissed her now. 'I have a surprise.' He rose from the sofa and crossed over to a bureau by the window. Then, throwing her a tantalising wink over his shoulder, he carefully opened the drawer.

Just for a moment Camilla's heart stilled as he drew out a carved wooden box with a silver lock and key.

'Don't worry.' He smiled at her, anticipating her reaction. 'It's not the *Ceò do dh'òr*. That's still safely back on Mhoire, where it belongs and where it will stay.'

Camilla smiled and breathed again as he came to sit beside her once more, remembering how Ross himself, as soon as her pregnancy had been confirmed, had insisted that the jewels be returned to a safe place on the island. 'One day our son will be the heir, and although I don't mind taking risks on my own behalf there's no way I'll endanger him. Besides,' he had added, holding her close, 'I know that you'll rest easier if the jewels are returned to Mhoire.'

That, she knew, had been the real reason, for she still entertained a slight lingering doubt as to whether the curse existed or not. The accident with the tractor, it had been proved, had indeed been caused by an electrical fault, just as Ross had claimed from the start. And Ross had reached his thirty-fifth birthday safely, without further incident, despite the jewels being at Castle Crannach.

Maybe the whole thing really was hokum, after all. But who knows? she'd insisted superstitiously, and to please her Ross had returned them to the island—just one of the countless thoughtful gestures that he had made to her over the past blissful year. For all his wild impetuosity, she had rapidly come to recognise that her husband was a caring and responsible man. Beneath that unconventional exterior he was as solid and dependable as a rock.

Her rock. She could count on that.

Now she waited as he turned the key of the box and, tantalisingly slowly, lifted the lid. The grey eyes sparkled as her own eyes widened. 'It's a replica! You've had them copied!' she gasped. For there, on a bed of deep blue velvet, lay three exquisite, identical copies of the ring, the necklace and the bracelet that had once belonged to Queen Margaret of Scotland.

First Ross lifted out the bracelet, flashing with garnets and lapis lazuli, and slid it on to her wrist. Then, brushing back her shiny blonde hair, he fastened the necklace around her throat. 'Come to the mirror and see how it looks,' he told her as he slipped on the ring.

He led her to the huge gilt-framed mirror that hung against the silk-covered wall, but just as last time when she had worn the real things, looking back at her she could see only his handsome face. She turned to him and looked up into his eyes, feeling her poor heart burst with love for him.

'Thank you.' She kissed him. 'Thank you, Ross, for everything.'

With a sigh, Ross gathered her into his arms. 'Never thank me,' he told her. 'Just love me.'

'I do, I do. You know I do.'

'And I love you.' He kissed her hair. 'Love of my life. My impossible dream.'

For a long moment they stood together, wrapped

blissfully in each other's arms. Then they went upstairs together, to the nursery, to see their son.

Six exciting series for you every month... from Harlequin

H A R L E Q U I N
American Romance®
Harlequin celebrates the American woman...

...by offering you romance stories written about American women, by American women for American women. This series offers you contemporary romances uniquely North American in flavor and appeal.

◆

H A R L E Q U I N
Temptation®

Passionate stories for today's woman

An exciting series of sensual, mature stories of love...dilemmas, choices, resolutions... all contemporary issues dealt with in a true-to-life fashion by some of your favorite authors.

◆

Harlequin Intrigue®
Because romance can be quite an adventure

Harlequin Intrigue, an innovative series that blends the romance you expect... with the unexpected. Each story has an added element of intrigue that provides a new twist to the Harlequin tradition of romance excellence.

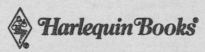

Harlequin Books®

PROD-A-2R